Darcy's Runaway Bride

Abbey North

Published by Abbey North JAFF Books, 2022.

DARCY'S RUNAWAY BRIDE

First edition. July 31, 2022.

Copyright © 2022 Abbey North.

ISBN: 979-8215207949

Written by Abbey North.

Blurb

A moment of madness causes Lizzy and Fitzwilliam to be compromised. They reluctantly wed, but he believes she conspired with her mother to force the union. Under those circumstances, they will never make a marriage work, so she agrees to his plan to pursue an annulment in three years. Lizzy is humiliated but determined to live her life as though Mr. Darcy isn't part of it...and he isn't.

Nearly four years later, an irate Fitzwilliam has come to America in search of his wayward bride. He wants to secure the annulment, so he follows her to the Colonies after she moves there when her sister marries an American. Bingley is along, and he doesn't hide his disapproval of Fitzwilliam's plan. When he finds Lizzy, she's quick to agree to the annulment as planned, so they undertake a journey to the nearest city to find legal counsel.

Along the way, their wagon wheel breaks, and they are set upon by bandits. Barely escaping, Lizzy is perilously injured, and Fitzwilliam has to find them help. A trapper and his family come to their aid, but as Lizzy heals, he realizes he can't imagine living without her. Will Lizzy give him a second chance, or is she determined to end their marriage that has never really begun?

Prologue

Considering how insufferable Fitzwilliam Darcy could be, Lizzy didn't like finding herself in the position of being grateful to spend time with him, but here they were. With Mr. Collins continuously hovering around her, she'd immediately accepted Mr. Darcy's invitation to dance. Now, she danced with him, keeping her gaze averted from his and not speaking.

"You seem sullen tonight, Miss Bennet. Is something troubling you?"

Her mouth dropped open in an O of surprise at the charge. "I am hardly sullen, Mr. Darcy, but it is frightfully rude of you to say so."

His lips quirked slightly. "As we both know, I am frightfully rude, am I not?"

In spite of herself, Lizzy's lips twitched at his self-deprecating comments. He clearly referenced the poor impression he'd made upon everyone at the Assembly ball upon first arriving in Meryton to visit with the Bingleys at Netherfield.

"I suppose it would be frightfully rude of me to disagree with you." She gave him an overly simpering smile, feeling chills down her spine when he chuckled unexpectedly. She softened her tone slightly, mainly because she didn't wish to be overheard. "I must thank you for your impulsive rescue, Mr. Darcy."

He cast a knowing glance in the direction of Mr. Collins, who was currently treading on poor Charlotte's feet. "He did seem to be quite attached to you."

Lizzy shuddered. "Yes. I fear he might be planning something dreadful."

Mr. Darcy's eyebrows furrowed into a deep V. "You believe him to be dishonorable?"

Lizzy shook her head. "Even worse. I suspect he has fully honorable intentions toward me. No doubt, he will soon propose, and I find myself feeling rather pitiable about the fact."

He frowned. "That should please your mother." The words came out starched and with a hint of coldness.

She frowned at his reaction. "Perhaps, but it shall not please me. I must find an alternative." She looked at him again, where he danced with Charlotte, and an idea started to occur to her. "My dear friend Charlotte feels she's been left on the shelf for too long. It seems as though she would welcome the attentions of a man like Mr. Collins."

"You would not wish to interfere with your mother's grand scheme." The words were relatively innocuous, though the tone was anything but.

Lizzy looked away from her friend and Mr. Collins to meet Mr. Darcy's gaze again. "You seem to be trying to say something, Mr. Darcy. I suggest you state it bluntly rather than tiptoe around it."

If he was surprised by her slightly snappish tone, he gave no indication. "I simply point out how much your mother likes to scheme to pair up her daughters. Not ten minutes ago, I heard her advising your sister Jane on how she must ensnare Mr. Bingley and keep his attention. After all, he does have four thousand per year." He spoke in a mocking tone.

She groaned softly. "My mother can be quite the burden sometimes, Mr. Darcy." Her eyes narrowed as she saw traces of his anger. "Surely, you do not believe Jane is like my mother?"

He turned his head to where Jane and Mr. Bingley stood on the edge of the dance floor, talking softly. Or at least they appeared to be. To Lizzy, it seemed quite an intimate pose, or as intimate as one could get in a ballroom surrounded by others. Her sister's cheeks were flushed and probably from pleasure rather than the heat generated by so many bodies crammed into a room together. "Is that supposed to make some sort of point, sir?"

He arched a brow. "She does not seem to regard him in an overly affectionate manner. I daresay, she would be speaking with any other companion with equal excitement and animation. Perhaps she has a slight preference for Bingley over someone like Mr. Collins, but I suspect the preference comes from annual income rather than the person himself."

She gasped at his accusation. "Are you implying Jane does not care about Bingley, and she is only trying to garner his attention for his income?"

He looked at her, his shoulders tense. He nodded once briskly. "I do not imply it, for there is no need. Instead, I state it bluntly as you requested when this conversation began."

Anger surged in Lizzy, and she had to stifle the urge to stomp on his foot. It wasn't necessarily out of concern for him, or even how poorly it would reflect on her own behavior, that stopped her. Rather, she suspected she would sustain far more pain from the action due to the thin soles of her dance slippers than he would with his feet clad in Hessians. "You have no idea what you are saying, Mr. Darcy. Jane loves Mr. Bingley."

He snorted. "They have known each other but a few weeks. It is impossible to love anyone in that short span of time."

Lizzy gritted her teeth. "Perhaps for more complicated people, but Jane is rather straightforward, as is your friend, Mr. Bingley. I believe they are a sound match."

"I believe you are mistaken. You are giving far too much credit to Miss Bennet's feelings."

"And you are giving no credit to them." Lizzy stopped dancing, finding she could no longer go through the motions. A couple nearby jostled into them at the unexpected stop and departure from decorum, but Lizzy was beyond caring. She clenched her hands into fists at her side, preparing to unleash her anger on Darcy when he did the worst thing possible.

He simply turned and walked away. He didn't give her an opportunity to vent her spleen or to defend her sister. The arrogant, overbearing nature of the man prickled Lizzy's temper, and she found herself storming after him. Even when he left the ballroom, she followed along behind, catching up with him in the hallway. She put her hand on his arm, and he flinched away from it, but he turned to face her.

"I am quite finished with our conversation, madam."

"I am not, Mr. Darcy. You are unfairly judging Jane. She is shy and reserved. She is not accustomed to showing her emotions, but she clearly lights up around Mr. Bingley. If you were not so blindly prejudiced toward her because of our family and lesser standing, you would see that as well."

"I am not prejudiced toward her. I can merely see as an independent observer that she does not love Bingley the way he should be loved. He deserves a love match, not one that is strictly one-sided. That kind of relationship might make him happy in the short term, but how could it ever possibly satisfy him for a lifetime?"

"It is not one-sided." She made no effort to modulate her tone or words. "You are as insufferable as I always believed you to be, Mr. Darcy."

"And you are as shrewish and ill-mannered as the rest of your family."

Lizzy lifted her hand to slap him before she could think better of it. She wasn't certain if she was irritated or relieved when his hand intercepted her wrist, keeping her from connecting her palm against his cheek. Her eyes widened at her display of passionate temper, for it wasn't like her at all. The man could draw out the worst in her, and she struggled to take a deep breath, trying to restore calm.

They stared at each other for a moment without speaking. His hand remained around her wrist, but it was a gentle hold, not a punishing one. It was only strong enough to keep her from slapping him, and when she slackened her shoulders and relaxed her aggressive pose, his grip further loosened, though he didn't completely release her.

As she stared into his deep brown eyes, Lizzy's mouth went dry. Her palms were sweaty, and her stomach clenched as something sparked to life in her breast. It caused a fluttering sensation she'd never experienced before, and she swore her heart was galloping faster than any of her father's plow horses could ever hope to.

"Miss Elizabeth..." He trailed off with a soft sigh, and his thumb started to stroke the inside of her palm where it rested around her wrist.

Lizzy shivered and closed her eyes for a moment at the sensation. It was barely anything, little more than a slight brush of his thumb against her skin, but it seemed like everything that mattered in the world distilled down to the simple touch. Her lips parted in a gasp as she stared up at him, seeing how tender and warm his gaze had become. She knew she should still be angry with him, but she couldn't seem to summon the will to be so. As his head bent toward hers to initiate a kiss, Lizzy relaxed, arching her head upward to meet him.

His lips pressed against hers in a gentle fashion, and though Lizzy had never been kissed before, she was certain kisses weren't normally like this. Surely, they couldn't be so earth-shattering and all-consuming? The kiss was changing her life, sharply delineating between the Before Lizzy, who'd never experienced anything like it, and the After Lizzy, who would never forget it.

He groaned as he pulled her closer, releasing her wrist to wrap his arms around her. Lizzy twined her arms around his neck and surrendered to the mastery of his mouth. His tongue had just shyly dipped into her mouth, and she was stroking it with equal reticence, when they were jerked apart by a crow of delight.

Fanny Bennet clapped her hands together as she caught them embracing. "Oh, this is wonderful indeed, Lizzy. You are such a clever girl. No wonder you have resisted my attempts to match you with Mr. Collins. No doubt, you realized all along you had Mr. Darcy well in hand."

Lizzy yanked away from Mr. Darcy at the same time he reared back. He looked incensed, and she was deeply ashamed by her mother's behavior, and by being caught in a tryst with him. "Mother, you do not know what you are saying."

"Do I not? It is quite obvious Mr. Darcy must now offer for your hand. Oh, what a brilliant idea you had, Lizzy. I could not have designed a more perfect plan."

Lizzy's mouth dropped open, and she slanted a glance at Mr. Darcy, who clearly reached the wrong conclusion. His lips tightened, and he glared at her. "I did not."

He held up a hand in an imperious fashion. "Save it, Miss Bennet. I assure you, your machinations will not work."

Fanny surged forward, hands on her hips. "What are you saying, Mr. Darcy? Do you intend to ruin my daughter? I assure *you*, you shall be ruining yourself and your reputation as well. Do you not have a young sister? What kind of example do you set for her by kissing innocents in dark corridors?"

Mr. Darcy flushed, his cheeks turning a ruddy color, and it was difficult to tell if he was more ashamed or infuriated. "I refuse to fall into Miss Bennet's trap."

Lizzy glared at him. "There was no trap, Mr. Darcy."

He arched a brow, clearly disbelieving. "And yet your mother commends you on your scheming. I suspect you are far more like her than I presumed. Such a pity."

"You will make an offer for her, or I will make such a scene that it will haunt you all the way back to London, Mr. Darcy." Fanny spoke coldly as she faced off with the man.

Lizzy was trying to defuse the situation, but instead she groaned as her father appeared then, looking troubled. "What has happened?"

"Nothing," said Lizzy quickly.

"Hardly nothing. I caught this man kissing our daughter in the darkened hallway here, Thomas. Can you imagine the uncouth behavior of one who is supposed to be a fine gentleman?"

Mr. Bennet stepped forward in a protective fashion, clearly angry. "Lizzy, was he forcing his attentions upon you?"

It didn't seem prudent to lie, for she was certain it would only make things worse. "No, Papa." She hazarded a glance at Mr. Darcy, who was looking vaguely like an ice sculpture at this point. "It was just a moment of madness, and it meant nothing."

"It means you are engaged, or he is a scoundrel." Fanny nodded for emphasis.

Mr. Bennet turned to Mr. Darcy. "Well, Darcy, will you be doing the right thing, or must I call you out?"

Lizzy's eyes widened, and she stepped forward. "Papa, you cannot call out Mr. Darcy for this. Literally, it was nothing. Mama has read too much into the situation."

Mr. Darcy stepped forward then. "Do not bother, Miss Bennet. For that would surely waste all your careful scheming and machinations. You have gotten what you desired. You must consider me a better catch than Mr. Collins to have stooped to this, so I will offer for your hand. We must have this distasteful business concluded as quickly as possible, for I want this kept as quiet as we can."

Lizzy shook her head. "I shall not marry you."

"You will, or your sisters will be ruined," said Fanny in a tone that was half-threatening and half-fretful. "You must do the right thing here, Lizzy."

It seemed patently obvious to her that the right thing was to forget all about the insane moment that had passed between her and Mr. Darcy and go their separate ways, but it was apparent neither of her parents were going to accept that idea.

Her father looked deeply unhappy as he scowled at Darcy. "I doubt you can arrange for a special license, so surely you will acquire one via the banns?"

Darcy's lip curled. "Hardly. I cannot think to draw out this matter for an additional three weeks. I will see the vicar at your local church and obtain a regular license." He turned and looked at Lizzy, his expression and tone revealing nothing but cold disdain. "We shall marry in one week, Miss Bennet. May you be happy with the schemes you have designed and the consequences you reap." With those words, he turned and walked away from them without another sound.

Lizzy glared after him before turning to face her parents. "Please, you cannot make this happen. It was an accident."

Fanny laughed. "An accident, dear? What, you stumbled into his lips? I am not naïve, dear girl."

"It was a temporary aberration. Why, just before the kiss, we had been arguing. Surely, Papa, you do not wish me to be married to someone with whom I disagree all the time?"

Mr. Bennet scowled. "No, I do not, but I suppose Darcy is correct in one regard. You must endure the consequences of your actions, and that goes for both of you. I am sorry, my dear, for it pains me greatly to imagine you marrying that odious man, but you must think of your sisters as well."

Lizzy frowned. "No one even knows about it except for you two and myself, along with Mr. Darcy. I assure you, neither he nor I will say anything."

Fanny's delighted smile made it obvious she wasn't going to agree with that. "Yet, word will still leak out. It is practically guaranteed, and then you will be ruined, and Mr. Darcy will be shamed as no true gentleman for not following through on his promises." She seemed almost as delighted about that outcome as she did at the idea of Lizzy marrying a man who made ten thousand per year.

Flustered and annoyed, and recognizing her mother's subtle threats, Lizzy threw her hands in the air and stormed away from them. She was angry and shaken, but she was determined there must be a way out. She wasn't going to marry Fitzwilliam Darcy. The idea was preposterous.

True, they might have engaged in some softening toward each other during her time at Netherfield while tending to Jane, but that was hardly the basis for a good relationship. He had blatantly accused Jane of being a gold-digger in all but name only, and he believed she'd engineered this. He would be no happier with her than she would be with him, and surely, once he calmed down, they could set aside their differences long enough to work together to find a solution that extricated them from an unwanted betrothal that would lead to nothing but an unhappy marriage.

DESPITE HER BEST EFFORTS to stop it, Lizzy found herself standing beside Fitzwilliam Darcy a week later at the church in Meryton. It was a small turnout, and there was no wedding breakfast scheduled to celebrate their union afterward. Mr. Darcy repeated his vows at the behest of the vicar, saying them in a cold and clipped fashion. It made the vicar cringe, but he didn't say anything.

When it was Lizzy's turn, she adopted the same terse tone and deliberately omitted the word obey from her repetition. The vicar shot her a look, and she glared back at him, daring him to comment. Apparently, he thought better of it, for he buried his attention back in his Bible, said the final prayer, and announced they were man and wife. When he invited Mr. Darcy to kiss the bride, Lizzy turned her head away, but she could see from the corner of her eye that Mr. Darcy had no intention of claiming the kiss anyway, for he quickly stepped back.

Together, they walked down the aisle, but they weren't touching. There was enough distance to fit another person between them, and it was surely as uncomfortable to be in the audience as it was to be a participant of the sham of a wedding.

Lizzy drew in a deep breath when she stepped out into the cold November air. A blanket of new snow covered the ground, and it was perfect for a beautiful winter wedding, except there was nothing beautiful about this farce. She turned to him. "What now, Mr. Darcy?"

"It is quite simple, Miss Bennet. I shall go a separate way from you, and in three years, we will reunite long enough to obtain an annulment. I assume you understand it is incumbent upon you to retain proof that we qualify for an annulment?"

It took Lizzy a moment to grasp what he meant, but then she gasped in outrage. "I am hardly likely to thwart my only opportunity to be free of you, Mr. Darcy."

"Excellent. In that case, let us proceed." He nodded to her and departed for his carriage. Lizzy walked away, joining her parents and sisters. They were obviously startled that she wasn't riding with her new husband.

"What is all this?" asked Fanny as Lizzy started to step into the carriage.

With her foot on the step, she turned to look at her mother. "It is our only alternative, Mama. Neither Mr. Darcy nor I wish to be shackled to each other, so we will abide for the next three years before we can obtain an annulment."

Fanny paled, grasping her chest. "What?" She shook her head insistently. "No, you cannot. You must fix this, Elizabeth Bennet. If you do not, we will be ruined. Your sisters will be ruined."

"My sisters have exactly three years to make sound matches, Mama, and as for fixing it, that is impossible." Lizzy glared at her mother for a moment. "If you had not insisted on and blackmailed your way to this outcome, we could have fixed it by forgetting the whole situation had ever occurred. What happens next must be firmly borne by you, Mama."

As she slipped past her father, who held the door, she was certain she detected a gleam of pride in his expression. Their relationship had been cooler of late, since he'd learned of her actions with Mr. Darcy, but perhaps he was now realizing she hadn't fundamentally changed who she was. They were all still paying for her momentary lapse of control though, Mr. Darcy included, who had been an equally willing participant. It was an unhappy turn of events, but things could hardly get worse.

LIZZY HAD CAUSE TO regret that conclusion later in the afternoon when Jane burst into their room, tears streaming down her face. "Dear sister, what is wrong?"

Jane tugged at a sodden handkerchief in her hand as she tried to gain control of herself long enough to speak. "It is dreadful, Lizzy. Just dreadful."

Lizzy had no idea what had her sister so distressed, but she rushed forward to put her arm around her waist. "What is dreadful?"

"Mr. Darcy has departed Netherfield."

Lizzy shrank internally for a moment, humiliated at being abandoned the very day of her wedding, but she was mostly relieved. She certainly hadn't expected him to stay around while they passed the three years until they could be free of each other. She would simply have to endure the gossip and humiliation, which would surely die down at some point. She hoped.

"Are you not hearing me, Lizzy?" Jane sounded frustrated, which was a rare state for her.

Lizzy patted her shoulder. "I am, Jane, but I am not surprised. He had announced to me his intention for us to go our separate ways, and though I did not realize that meant he would leave Netherfield so quickly, I am not overly upset."

"I am." Jane dissolved into a fresh round of tears.

Lizzy patted her shoulder. "Truly, Jane, there is no love lost between the man and me. I am not heartbroken that he has chosen to turn away from me and pursue an annulment."

"You do not understand, dear Lizzy. He is taking the Netherfield party with him."

Lizzy frowned, certain she must have misunderstood. "What?"

"Our lady's maid heard it from a footman, who is friends with a footman at Netherfield. They are packing up the entire Bingley and Darcy party, and they will be departing in the morning. I am sorry for how it has ended for you, but this also means it is over for me. Mr. Bingley is leaving, and I will not see him again." Jane started to cry again.

Lizzy drew her into her arms, rocking her sister. She wondered if she could approach Darcy and try to talk sense into him, but she already knew that would be futile. His opinion of Jane likely hadn't changed in the last week, because he had no desire to reevaluate it and allow it to do so. If Bingley was the type to be cowed into leaving with Darcy, Lizzy consoled herself with the thought that he didn't deserve Jane anyway.

Of course, Jane was unlikely to see that point-of-view, so Lizzy kept all counsel and words to herself. Instead, she muttered soothing sounds of comfort while she rubbed her sister's back and accepted Jane's torrent of tears. Remorse filled her, for her careless lapse, followed by Fanny's machinations, had led to her having an unwanted husband. Even worse, it was costing Jane the possibility of a much-desired husband, one whom she would love and be happy with, unlike Lizzy, should she have been forced to remain as Mr. Darcy's bride.

Chapter One

June 1815, Ohio

Fitzwilliam's lip curled as they entered the town of Prosperity, Indiana. It hardly lived up to its name, but he had expected little from an American settlement. This trip had been nothing but one inconvenience after another, and he was relieved to finally be nearing the end of it.

"Are you certain this is the right course, Darcy?" asked Bingley, who had insisted on accompanying him when he'd departed from England several months ago to track down his errant bride.

Fitzwilliam slanted his friend a disbelieving look. "I am quite positive, Bingley. Do you honestly believe I would have traveled across the ocean, endured the American transport system, taken that flatboat down the Ohio River, and then traveled all this way on horse if I were not sure?"

Bingley looked chastened, and he nodded. "No, I suppose not." He heaved a sigh. "We are here now, so you can conclude your business quickly." He was obviously trying to attempt to hide his disapproval, but he wasn't all that good at screening his emotions.

Darcy felt the sting of his friend's unspoken criticism, but he didn't reply. It didn't matter if Bingley approved of his plan to annul the marriage with Elizabeth Bennet. What mattered was finding the woman, obtaining her cooperation, and returning to Pemberley as soon as possible. He'd been away far too long as it was and traveling to the wilds of America was hardly the way he wished to spend his time.

"I should have insisted she must remain where I put her before I left," he grumbled partially under his breath.

Bingley sent him a look. "Chap, you could hardly expect her to remain where she was, and she can hardly be faulted for not maintaining contact to apprise you of her movements when you made no effort to ensure she was comfortable or safe."

Fitzwilliam frowned at his friend. "She and I had an understanding, Bingley. I am certain she reached the conclusion that her scheming would not work, and so she decided to be graceful about it."

Bingley muttered something, but Fitzwilliam didn't bother to inquire what. He was certain it would be a condemnation of his handling of the whole matter. He couldn't say Bingley had harped on him over the last few years, but his friend occasionally mentioned it or asked about Miss Bennet's state of health. Fitzwilliam never had an answer for him, because he didn't maintain contact. Of course, he was certain Bingley was far more interested in hearing about Miss Jane than he was about Miss Elizabeth. Even after all this time, Bingley still seemed to have a *tendre* for her.

"I do not know where to find her, so we shall have to ask." He'd engaged a Runner about a year before, as the three years had ticked past. He had been forced to do so after turning up at Longbourn and discovering everything had completely changed. Mr. Collins and his wife, Charlotte Collins, had been installed then, and he'd learned Mr. Bennet had passed away two years ago.

It had taken a while to get Mrs. Collins to admit Elizabeth Bennet was in America. Fitzwilliam had been annoyed by that, and further annoyed when the woman refused to tell him anything more, even with the pressure her husband applied. His Runner had tracked her here, but he had no concrete details on how to find her beyond the town of Prosperity.

There were few buildings erected. They were closest to the sheriff's office, and there was a tavern. On the other side of the street, there was a sign labeled "Boarding House," and he veered in that direction. He wanted no part of the tavern, which likely had rooms available, but seemed seedy and was an unseemly place for him and Bingley to enter.

When they stepped into the boarding house, Fitzwilliam was afraid they might be attacked by doilies. They seemed to cover every square inch of the place, and it served to create a stifling atmosphere.

A plump older woman bustled in from another room to greet them. "Hello, gentlemen. Are you here for a room?"

"We are here for information," said Fitzwilliam.

"And perhaps some food, if you offer that service," said Bingley as he inhaled appreciatively. "Something smells delicious."

The older woman blushed at his exuberant compliment. "I do not normally serve to those who are not guests, but I suppose I can make an exception. What is it I can do for you gentlemen?" She looked at them for a moment as though she was sizing them up. "I am Martha Freely. This is my establishment."

"I am Charles Bingley, and this is my associate, Fitzwilliam Darcy." Bingley stepped forward, offering his most charming smile. Though he had been traveling just as long and as hard as Fitzwilliam, he appeared far less affected by the stresses of the road.

"My friend is looking for someone. We were directed to Prosperity, but we do not know how to find her now." As he spoke, Bingley tucked the woman's arm through his and led her back the way she'd came, as though he'd been in the house many times before and knew its layout.

With a muttered sound of impatience, Fitzwilliam followed behind them. He didn't want to waste time with small talk or eating what promised to be relatively plain fare. Once they had left Boston, which was surprisingly civilized, there were fewer and fewer touches of elegance and sophistication along the way.

He found himself following them into a dining room, where there were two other guests seated at a long table. The food was already laid out, and his stomach rumbled in spite of himself. It was the basic fare he'd expected—some kind of fried meat, fried potatoes, biscuits, and white gravy—but he had been traveling long enough that the offerings weren't terribly unpleasant.

"Do sit down, gentlemen," said Mrs. Freely after Bingley had seen her to a chair.

Fitzwilliam sat down in one, doing his best to avoid sitting near the other guests.

"Who are you looking for?" asked the older woman after the dishes had been passed, she'd said grace, and they were starting to eat.

"A Miss Elizabeth Bennet." Fitzwilliam could scarcely imagine thinking of her as Elizabeth Darcy. To his knowledge, she'd not taken his name, and he hoped that was the case. To his way of thinking, she had no right to it, and fortunately, she seemed to have agreed.

Mrs. Freely frowned as though thinking for a moment, and then her expression brightened. "Yes, she lives on the Middlemeer farm. It is about half a day's ride from here, and it is getting late, gentlemen." She cast a meaningful look out the window, which displayed the bright sun of afternoon overhead.

"I am certain we will have plenty of time," said Fitzwilliam in a decisive fashion.

"It is rough territory, Mr. Darcy, and if you get stuck without finding them before nightfall, you shall be forced to make camp."

Fitzwilliam shuddered at the prospect. He'd had to do it more than once on this trip, including sleeping on the deck of a flatboat for several days, but he preferred to avoid such a fate. Once he returned to England, he would never again sleep anywhere but the finest beds that he already had at Darcy House and Pemberley. "That would be dreadful."

"I do have a room available with two beds. I am afraid I cannot offer you both a private room, gentlemen, but you are welcome to have it for the night if you wish. I can give you instructions for reaching your destination, and you can start out tomorrow morning with fresh provisions while being well-rested and possessing a sharper mind."

Fitzwilliam sighed as Bingley sent him a questioning look. What was another night in the scheme of things, since his three-year marriage was almost closer to four now? "Yes, I believe we will have the room, Mrs. Freely."

"Wonderful. You must tell me what brings you gentlemen here. It is obvious from your accent that you are not from around here."

"Are you Canadian?" asked one of the two younger guests seated at the table. The older one appeared to be around Fitzwilliam's age. He shook his head at the younger boy. "They are clearly British, Clancy."

"Yes, we have traveled from England." Fitzwilliam was content to leave it at that, so he let Bingley field the questions as they were pestered with them. He supposed he understood the fascination, particularly from the younger fellow, who'd probably never had much experience with anyone from England before, but he found it intrusive and somewhat gauche, just like the rest of the Americans with whom he'd interacted. Whatever had brought Lizzy to this godforsaken place?

When what they called dinner finally ended, he and Bingley went to the room they'd been assigned, but he stayed only long enough to remove his outer layer of clothing, since Bingley had requested a bath. Fitzwilliam would like to enjoy one as well, but he left his friend to privacy for the moment as he walked downstairs.

He was uncertain what to do with himself, but the boardinghouse offered no answers, so he left it and walked slowly down the single street of town. He could see sheaves of wheat blowing in the distance, and he was surrounded by nothing but monotonous flatness. There had been mountains earlier in their journey, but this place seemed to be nothing but a straight line with an occasional hill.

Once again, he found himself wondering how Miss Bennet had ended up in such a place. He was quite annoyed that he'd had to track her for so long, but he dared hope they could conclude their business quickly, and he could be back in England before Christmas.

THEY LEFT MRS. FREELY'S boardinghouse the next morning packed with the provisions she'd promised, along with a hand-drawn map. He had to admit the woman had skill for it, and he felt reasonably confident they could find the Middlemeer farm just by following her directions.

Though it was June, it was early enough in the morning to have a slight chill in the air, and he briefly wondered if he had made a mistake by refusing to purchase a leather duster similar to the one Mr. Bingley wore. He'd obtained it in Portsmouth, along with a bowler hat. Fitzwilliam was still perfectly content with his top hat, thank you very much, and he saw no reason to dress like the Americans, but he had to admit his fine tweed jacket wasn't quite as warm as Bingley's duster obviously was.

As the day wore on, he was glad he had not picked up such a garment though. Bingley had to pause within an hour of them setting out so he could strip off the duster and tuck it in his saddle bags. Then they had proceeded, riding for hours. Fitzwilliam had endured the heat as it built, and now he was sweating lightly, but he refused to stop and remove his jacket. It would be unseemly, and he declined to have the Americans looking down upon him.

It was with some relief they saw a sprawling set of buildings far ahead of them, surrounded by timber fencing. The gate was open, so they rode through without stopping, and then they rode. And rode. And rode.

Fitzwilliam was starting to think they were either lost, or perhaps Mrs. Freely had deliberately misguided them, for the endless path seemed like it would never end. Just when he was certain they were trapped on this perfectly flat road that would continue until their lives ended, he could finally see the structures they'd viewed from a distance appearing closer.

In his eagerness, Fitzwilliam tapped his spur lightly against the horse, encouraging it to speed up. Bingley easily matched pace, and they soon arrived at what appeared to be the primary residence, since it was the largest building, save for a barn a few hundred feet in the distance.

Bingley appeared invigorated, and Fitzwilliam didn't have to wonder why. His friend was obviously excited about the possibility of seeing Jane Bennet again. From what the Runner had gathered, Miss Jane resided with Miss Elizabeth here, along with their mother, and two of their other sisters.

He removed his top hat as Bingley took off his bowler, and they approached the door. He rapped firmly against it, and it opened a moment later. A woman who had to be in her mid-forties stood there staring at both of them for a moment. "Yes? How may I help you gentlemen?"

"We are here to see Miss Jane Bennet," blurted out Bingley with obvious excitement. "Err, Miss Elizabeth Bennet."

The housekeeper eyed both for a moment, and Fitzwilliam had the strange thought they might not pass muster with the woman.

"And who might you be?" she asked.

"I am Charles Bingley, and this is my friend, Fitzwilliam Darcy." The woman gasped softly, and she reached forward to push open the screen door, inviting them in. She let Bingley through without problem, but Fitzwilliam swore for a moment she was going to let the door slam in his face.

Instead, she stepped back with an ill-concealed huff and gestured for him to come in. She closed the door behind them and said, "Follow me, and I will take you where you can wait for them." She led them down the hall to a sitting room and gestured for them to sit. "I shall see that the ladies join you shortly. May I offer you tea or coffee while you wait?"

"Nothing," said Fitzwilliam decisively.

"Tea," said Bingley at the same time, before adding, "Or coffee is fine if that is what you have available. We do not want to cause you any trouble."

The housekeeper clearly liked Mr. Bingley, for she grinned at him. "It is no trouble, so which would you prefer, young man?"

"Nothing," said Fitzwilliam again.

The housekeeper barely glanced at him and then beamed her approval when Bingley said, "I would not mind a spot of coffee."

Fitzwilliam shook his head, shocked that his friend had embraced the philistine beverage. It was nothing like tea, but Bingley seemed to have taken to it.

The woman disappeared, and Fitzwilliam sat with discomfort in a small, spindly chair. He didn't speak or look up until he heard a rustling sound in the doorway, and he braced himself for his first sight of Elizabeth Bennet in nearly four years.

It was somewhat of a letdown when Miss Jane crossed the doorway instead. She stared at them for a moment, hands clasped to her mouth. She seemed on the verge of tears, but her voice emerged unexpectedly cool and distant when she said, "I could scarcely believe we had visitors from England when Mrs. Tucker announced it to me. Yet here you are." There was a faint hint of chastisement underlaying her words. "What an unexpected surprise to see both of you here." She walked into the sitting room at an unhurried pace, taking a chair by the fireplace and away from them. "What brings you here?"

"We are here to—"

"I shall discuss that with Miss Elizabeth, Miss Bennet," said Darcy in a repressive tone as he glared at his friend.

Her nose wrinkled, but she didn't reply to him. Instead, she turned her attention to Bingley.

As he waited for Elizabeth Bennet, he couldn't help observing Miss Jane interacting with his friend. There still seemed to be a spark, at least on his friend's side. He had to concede Miss Jane was blushing in a becoming fashion, and she clearly seemed pleased to see Bingley, though she was holding herself somewhat aloof as well.

His thoughts about Miss Jane, and his concerns about Bingley getting involved with her again, fled his mind when Miss Elizabeth appeared at the doorway. She hovered for a moment, as though trying to decide whether she wanted to come in. Finally, with a sigh he heard even from where he sat, she entered.

He hadn't sipped his coffee, and he was grateful for it, so he had nothing on which to choke that way. He hadn't seen her in so long that she was practically a different person in some ways. Her hair, which had once been worn in an elegant twist, was now confined by an elegant bun, and she had slimmed a bit while still retaining a pleasing roundness. With gracefulness, she swept across the room and took a wingback near his as he stood in a show of respect before sitting down after her.

"Hello, Miss Bennet."

She inclined her head. "Hello. What are you doing here?"

So, there would be few pleasantries, if any. That suited him fine. "This has been a long journey, and I hoped we might speak in private, Miss Bennet."

She hesitated for a moment before nodding. As she stood up, he realized there was a trace of dust on her nose. He was unable to stifle the impulse to retrieve the handkerchief from his pocket as he got to his feet as well. He moved closer and wiped it from her nose for her, touching his as he explained, "You had a bit of dust there."

She didn't seem all that surprised. "We have been cleaning the pantry." She shrugged a shoulder. "Follow me."

As they walked past Bingley and Miss Jane, Fitzwilliam stiffened at the sight of Fanny Bennet entering. She eyed him with beady-eyed appraisal, and he couldn't help feeling she was seeing pound notes instead of his visage. She looked happy for a moment, and then her expression turned grim. She'd obviously realized why he was there, and it must have surprised her. Did she really think he would have allowed himself to remain leg-shackled to her daughter indefinitely?

"What an unexpected surprise, Mr. Darcy. And you as well, Mr. Bingley." Fanny's voice was considerably warmer when she spoke to Bingley than when she spoke to Fitzwilliam.

For a moment, he'd been on the verge of reconsidering his decision, since Miss Elizabeth looked so good after all this time, and her scent was still as unique and pleasant as ever. Seeing Fanny Bennet reminded him of the circumstances of their unwanted union though, and he straightened his backbone as he followed Lizzy from the room. He would only leave once he had an annulment, and not a second before.

Chapter Two

Lizzy loathed the betraying flutter of excitement in her stomach at the first sight of Fitzwilliam Darcy. Part of her had believed she would never see him again, though she had known in the back of her mind he would find a way to her. He absolutely would not want to be tied to Lizzy longer than he must, which suited her fine.

She was annoyed with herself for still finding him attractive even in just a physical way, and she assured herself that was the only excitement that came from seeing him. That, and perhaps when she was free of him, she might choose to take a husband she could love.

Lizzy nearly snorted aloud at the thought. While there were many men who expressed interest in her, and even a few who would have been unscrupulous enough not to care that she was technically married, she had yet to meet a man who would tempt her to give up the freedom she enjoyed. Not even Mr. Darcy could have persuaded her to do that, but of course, she bore no love for him. It had simply been an aberrant attraction born out of contrariness in light of their mutual anonymity.

She led him into a sitting room and gestured for him to take a seat. "Would you like tea, Mr. Darcy?"

"That will not be necessary, Miss Bennet." His jaw looked tight, and she thought she must have imagined the temporary warmth he'd seemed to display upon their first reunion.

She braced herself to deal with an angry Fitzwilliam, finding she wasn't overly alarmed by the prospect. She reached for the bell and rang it despite his frown.

"I said I do not require tea."

"That is your prerogative, but I would like some, Fitzwilliam." She used his name deliberately to annoy him, and Lizzy had to bite the inside of her cheek to keep from giggling at the expected flash of irritation.

"Miss Bennet, I—"

"You might as well call me Elizabeth, or perhaps Lizzy, Fitzwilliam." She had to pause for a moment to greet Mrs. Tucker, who lingered in the doorway. "Would you please bring us tea, Mrs. Tucker?"

"Aye, Miss Bennet," said the housekeeper in her charming Irish brogue.

Mr. Darcy was frowning, and Lizzy chose to deliberately interpret it in a contrary fashion. "If you are wondering about Mrs. Tucker's accent, she is originally from Ireland. She was Jacob's nurse growing up, and so when he decided to come to America, she chose to accompany him."

"Fascinating." His tone indicated it was anything but. "I am not here to discuss the servants' lives, Miss Bennet."

"Jacob is hardly a servant, Fitzwilliam." She kept her tone pleasant, attempting to hide her amusement at his expense. There was something just plain fun about riling Mr. Darcy, and it always had been. "After all, he is dear Kitty's husband, and the second son of a baron. I am certain that matters most to you."

He let out a growl of frustration, but he was prevented from launching into a tirade by the return of Mrs. Tucker, who bore a tray. She placed it on the table near Lizzy, and there were two cups. She thanked the housekeeper and turned to Darcy again. "May I offer you a cup?"

"No, I do not want any bloody tea."

Lizzy had to bite her lip to keep from laughing outright. "There is hardly call for that kind of language, Fitzwilliam."

He muttered something, but then his face flushed, and he nodded tightly. "You are correct, Miss Bennet. I owe you an apology for vulgarity."

She waved a hand dismissively. "I live on a farm, and I can assure you I have heard worse, though inadvertently, of course." The men who worked the Ohio farm her brother-in-law owned were rougher chaps than she was used to, often using coarse language while engaged in their tasks, though they would never knowingly behave that way in front of Lizzy or her sisters or her mother. Despite their rough edges, she found them all quite likable, and she enjoyed some of the lesser formality between the household and staff that the Middlemeers practiced.

"Why did you run away, Elizabeth?" It seemed to pain him to use her first name, and he was still gritting his teeth.

She frowned. "I did not run away, Mr. Darcy, and you flatter yourself to think I did."

"So I am to be Mr. Darcy again? I do wish you would decide which form of address you plan to use, Miss Bennet."

She hid her smile behind the cup of tea before taking a sip. "If you insist, I am perfectly happy to use first names, for we are married." How she delighted in reminding him of that, simply because it so clearly irritated him. "Fitzwilliam."

He seemed on the verge of throwing his hands in the air and shouting his frustration for a moment, so it was admirable that he maintained control and had only the faintest hint of annoyance in his tone when he spoke. "You knew we could get an annulment in three years, and yet you moved to the wilds of the Colonies. Why have you run away from your obligation?"

She frowned. "My obligation? You made it quite clear you do not wish for me to engage in any of my obligations as your wife, Fitzwilliam. Not that I wish to have you engaged as my husband either." She hastily added that lest he got the wrong idea.

He snorted. "You certainly went to an awful lot of trouble while scheming with your mother to ensure that outcome if it was not your desire."

She glared at him, feeling her own irritation rise. "I understand what you believe about the matter, and I know the truth. I was not party to trying to trap you, Fitzwilliam, and I am happy to end this farce of a marriage." She used his first name again mostly to be irritating.

"That is indeed happy news, Elizabeth," he said with a clenched jaw. "I am heartened to realize you plan to cooperate with the endeavor, though you have forced me to travel all the way here and waste many months beyond when we could have been freed from each other."

"I know it might be difficult for you to grasp, but you truly did not enter my mind much at all when I made the decision to come with Kitty to America after she met and married Jacob while he was visiting his family in England. I daresay, you have scarcely entered my thoughts at all these many years, and I had completely lost track of when we were able to annul, or I would have sought out legal advice to begin the process on my side."

That wasn't entirely true. Lizzy had been well aware when three years had passed, and it had generated a faint buzz of awareness in the back of her mind that Mr. Darcy might reenter her life at any point after that, but she'd mostly tried to relegate him to the shadowy depths of the future, deciding he was a problem to deal with then.

His mouth tightened, but he sounded relatively pleasant when he said, "Then we are agreed. An annulment is the best way forward."

"We have been agreed about that since we were forced to exchange vows at the church." She sipped her tea again, mildly amused when he moved from his seat to pour himself a cup after a long moment. "I assume you have the paperwork?"

He scowled. "I did have, prepared by my solicitor before I departed on the ship bound for America. However, the flatboat that we took to reach Ohio flooded more than once, and the papers were destroyed. We must seek out a solicitor here to begin the process."

Lizzy frowned. "I do not believe we will have much luck locally, for Portsmouth is still quite small to have its own solicitor. And there is no one lurking about on Middlemeer land that might be able to assist us with this project."

He frowned. "I was afraid that might be the case. Will we be forced to return to Boston or somewhere somewhat civilized?"

Lizzy hesitated for a moment and then shook her head. "No, I believe we might be able to find someone who can assist us in Cincinnati. It is a couple days' travel from here, but what is two more days in the pursuit of being free?"

He was clearly annoyed by yet another setback, but he nodded after a moment. "Indeed, I suppose that is true. We shall leave tomorrow?"

Lizzy shook her head. "It will have to be at least the next day. I have many chores which I must attend tomorrow. Perhaps you and Mr. Bingley would like to assist us?" She asked the question with her brow arched, betraying her disbelief that he would accept such an idea.

Of course, he couldn't resist the challenge, and she wasn't surprised that he frowned at her and said, "Of course, we would be happy to assist."

Lizzy did her best to hide her smile. She had a difficult time imagining Mr. Darcy on a working farm. Mr. Bingley might be slightly more suited for the tasks, but he was still a full generation removed from trade, and he had grown up as a gentleman as well. She had no doubt they could handle the financial realities of managing such an estate, but she wasn't certain either man was up for the physical nature of the job involved. "I am certain Jacob will be happy to have your assistance, and then we can plan to travel the next day."

In truth, they could have traveled the very next day, but Lizzy wanted to allow Jane some extra time with Mr. Bingley in case Bingley planned to accompany them on the trip. She hadn't seen her sister so animated in years, and she was determined to give Jane another chance to prove to Mr. Bingley that she wanted to be with him. Lizzy could only assume that Fitzwilliam had been successful in persuading Bingley before that Jane's affections weren't true, but she hoped he would soon realize his friend had been wrong all those years ago.

LIZZY FOUND HERSELF seated across from Fitzwilliam that evening, and she was pleased to see Bingley had taken the seat beside Jane. They were currently engaged in quiet conversation, but it appeared animated. There was a sparkle in her sister's eyes and a flush in her cheeks that had been missing for too long. Lizzy was determined Mr. Darcy would not come between them again.

"Lizzy tells me you will be traveling to Cincinnati to handle legal matters," said Jacob from the head of the table. He was a blond man with slightly heavy features, a muscular build, and a look of utter adoration each time he glanced at Kitty. That hadn't changed since the day they'd met, and his obvious love for her sister was one of the things Lizzy liked best about Jacob.

"It is unfortunately a necessity due to the loss of the paperwork from the means of conveyance to reach here." Fitzwilliam scowled. "It is quite a difficult prospect to get here from civilization. How can you endure it?"

"I quite enjoy the country life." Jacob seemed unbothered by any criticism marring Fitzwilliam's tone. "It is not much different from the estate life in England, in truth."

"Anywhere in England, you can reach civilization with a reasonable amount of travel, and I much prefer a coach over a flatboat any day."

"Yes, but I consider that one of the charms of this area. We are still quite isolated and on our own. Whatever we accomplish is at our own hands." That was a topic Jacob was passionate about, and Lizzy was afraid he might launch into a full-scale praise of the frontier lifestyle.

She found his thoughts somewhat fascinating, but she'd heard them many times now.

She quickly interrupted Jacob before he could truly begin. "We travel to Cincinnati once or twice a year, and they generally have just about everything we need. I believe we are all content here, except perhaps Mama."

Fanny looked up, sending a censorious frown across the table to Lizzy. "I am quite content here, daughter. It is certainly better to live at Jacob's largesse than Mr. Collins.'" She smiled at her son-in-law beneficently. He had an uncanny way of being able to handle Fanny, and he'd won her over despite where he'd chosen to settle, and the lack of civilized comforts that Fanny pined over and talked about even years later.

"Yes, I had heard about Mr. Bennet's passing, though I am vague on the details. You have my condolences, Mrs. Bennet." Fitzwilliam spoke stiffly.

Fanny nodded graciously, though she'd made no attempt to hide her dislike of Darcy. "Thank you, Mr. Darcy."

"Yes, it was quite tragic." Mr. Bingley looked at Jane, his expression full of sorrow. "I am certain it must have been difficult for you, Miss Jane."

Jane nodded, blinking sharply for a minute. Her grief underscored Lizzy's own, and though it had settled into a quiet place that had become part of her, it was no less painful than it had been to remember losing her father.

"It is Kitty's fault," said Lydia in a sullen tone.

Kitty sighed, and Lizzy frowned at Lydia. It wasn't the first time her sister had made such a charge, and it was nonsense. "It is hardly Kitty's fault that she fell in love and moved to America. Nor is it her fault that Mama and Papa decided to come visit because Mama missed her daughter so. It is most certainly not Kitty or Jacob's fault that Papa contracted encephalitis."

Mr. Bingley frowned. "What a dreadful thing. Err, what is it?"

"It is a terrible swelling of the brain," said Fanny with a delicate sniff as she pulled a handkerchief from her sleeve and dabbed at her eyes. "My nerves can hardly stand it whenever I think about having to endure Thomas's decline."

Lizzy barely resisted the urge to roll her eyes. "I am quite certain it was even worse for Papa." Her mother had a singular knack for making everything about herself. There was no point in trying to change her though.

"I am certain Mr. Collins was fairly happy for the turn of events," said Lizzy after a moment. She shrugged. "Charlotte seems quite content as the mistress of Longbourn. We exchange letters once or twice a year, though the post can take several months, as you can well imagine."

"Did you know Mrs. Collins is expecting?" asked Fitzwilliam.

Lizzy turned her head to look at him, tilting it slightly in her surprise. "Is she?"

He nodded. "The Collins had come for a visit the last time I was in Kent to call on Lady Catherine. She is my aunt, if you did not know. Mrs. Collins was with child. I do not know when she was due, but that was a few months ago. It is quite likely she has given birth by now."

Lizzy smiled. "Then I surely have a letter coming from Charlotte in the next months to tell me all about her precious bundle." She felt a slight pang of envy. For the most part, Lizzy was content remaining single—though technically married right now, she considered herself single in all ways that counted—but that was one drawback to not marrying.

She would never have a family of her own, but she was quite content with her niece and nephew. Kitty's son, just barely out of leading strings, promised to be as willful as his mother, but perhaps as interesting too.

"What of your family, Mr. Bingley?" asked Jane. "How are your sisters? I did try writing to Miss Caroline a couple of times after you departed Netherfield, but I received no response."

Lizzy winced, remembering how devastated Jane had been. It had taken her sister the longest time to accept that Miss Caroline had not been the friend she had judged her to be.

"Louisa is doing quite well. She and her husband have welcomed a set of twins." Bingley smiled. "Jasper and Jamila are quite a handful between the two of them."

Jane smiled, seeming truly pleased for Mrs. Hurst. "How delightful."

"And Miss Bingley?" asked Lizzy, prompted by curiosity.

"She seems content enough." It was a brief answer that revealed nothing.

"Is she engaged or married?" Jane seemed to genuinely care.

Lizzy found herself interested. She couldn't help speculating that Caroline Bingley would hang on until Darcy was freed from his marriage to Lizzy by annulment.

"She is not," said Bingley. "Miss Georgiana is engaged though."

Lizzy dared to glance at Fitzwilliam, trying to gauge if he was pleased about that. He didn't seem displeased at least. "I do not believe we ever had the pleasure of meeting your sister, Mr. Darcy."

He nodded once. "She was in Pemberley at the time, safely protected."

She couldn't help feeling that was a subtle insult, implying she was protected from association with the Bennets. Her tone cooled in response. "I hope she has found a man who makes her quite happy."

"He is a colonel in the militia and a comrade of our cousin's."

"You find that an acceptable match, Fitzwilliam?" Lizzy didn't have to feign all her shock. "Surely, his connections are far too low to be allowed to join with your family?"

His lips tightened in irritation, and he seemed like he wouldn't answer for a moment. Finally, he said, "Georgiana genuinely loves him, and more importantly, it is obvious he loves her. I could not object to their joining when there was true love between them."

Lizzy glared at him for a moment, understanding he was implying that Jane still did not care about Bingley and never had. She took a deep breath to keep from lashing out, focusing her attention on Jane instead, relishing in her happiness.

Finally, dinner ended, though Lizzy was displeased that Jacob had invited Mr. Bingley and Mr. Darcy to stay until the matter was resolved. She wasn't surprised, for he would have felt like he must extend hospitality, particularly under the circumstances, but she'd rather enjoyed the thought of Mr. Darcy being forced to sleep by a campfire, or perhaps spread a bedroll in the bunkhouse.

She and Jane went up together later, after they'd all shared tea, going to their room. She helped Jane undress before Jane assisted her, and they were soon in their nightgowns and curled together in the bed, since it was cold in the room. Though it was warm throughout the day, it was starting to get cold at night, though it was just June. It wasn't quite cold enough to require a fire though.

"I am so happy, Lizzy. Mr. Bingley has returned to me, and he is not engaged or married. He was very fast to tell me that, within minutes of our speaking again."

Lizzy smiled, though her sister couldn't see it in the dark. "I suspect he is still as in love with you as he ever was, Jane. Obviously, you still have strong feelings for him."

"I do." Jane sounded doubtful though.

That made Lizzy frown. "Are you uncertain how you feel about him now?"

"No, it is the contrary. I am uncertain how he feels about me, or how he ever felt. I thought at the time he returned my affection, but he left Netherfield so easily without a word of parting, and he never wrote to me. I just do not know how he feels."

"You know he could not write to you, for etiquette would forbid it. He could no more send you letters than you could write to him unless you are engaged. You cannot hold it against Mr. Bingley that Caroline never responded to your missives. She was just as determined to drive you apart as Mr. Darcy was, so I doubt she ever told Bingley that you had been in contact."

Lizzy had told Jane that in the past, but it seemed important to remind her sister of the reasons why Bingley might not have reached out. Of course, there was no true justification for why he had been pressured to leave to start with, other than he lacked moral fiber and a strong spine to stand up for what he desired. She couldn't entirely blame him for that either, for Fitzwilliam Darcy was a formidable man, and it must be difficult to go against him—if one desired his good opinion, which she did not.

"I was most surprised to see Mr. Darcy turn up with Mr. Bingley."

"I am not," said Lizzy. "It does not surprise me at all that Mr. Bingley came along on the journey. Perhaps he is along to keep Fitzwilliam company, but likely, it is just as much to see you. Otherwise, it was quite an arduous journey to undertake only to keep a friend company."

Jane sounded optimistic. "I do hope you are right, Lizzy. I do not wish to have my heart broken again, so I am distrustful of the connection between myself and Mr. Bingley."

Lizzy considered it for a moment, trying to decide how to phrase her thoughts. "I believe some caution is warranted, for you do not wish to hand him your heart to crush once more, but do not be so overly cautious that you are afraid to let your natural feelings bloom again, particularly if they are clearly reciprocated."

Jane squeezed her hand in the dark. "You are so wise, Lizzy. What of you and Mr. Darcy?"

"We are to annul this farce of a union as planned." Lizzy was careful to keep any betrayal of emotion from her tone. It was the plan and always had been, and though she had been humiliated at the time of him abandoning her, she had endured.

She hadn't cared that he had gone, or that he believed she was conspiring with her mother to trap him into an unwanted union. Thinking of that only fueled her anger and made her glad he had left, and by the time she'd come to America, she was certain she had mostly forgotten about the man.

"But you call him Fitzwilliam?"

Lizzy giggled. "It is mostly to irritate him, dear Jane."

Jane sounded confused. "Why would you wish to irritate him?"

Lizzy struggled to explain before shrugging, though she wasn't certain Jane could feel the motion. "I do not know, other than it is quite good fun. No, that chapter of my life is nearly closed. We will travel to Cincinnati and obtain the means to be free of each other."

"Will you begin considering the courting offers you have received?" asked Jane.

Lizzy scoffed. "I am hardly likely to hand over my freedom. No, thank you. For my part, I am content to have everyone around here believe I remain married." She was quite decided on that, having reached the conclusion that afternoon that the pretense of being a married woman, even after her annulment went through, could be quite useful in keeping away persistent suitors.

"If you are certain, Lizzy." Jane sounded unsure though. "I shall come with you to Cincinnati as your chaperone."

Lizzy started to nod, and then she had another idea. "No, I do not believe you should do so. For one thing, you are needed here on the farm."

Jane sighed softly. "Yes, there is always more work than hands, but it would be improper to allow you to travel with Mr. Bingley and Mr. Darcy."

"I believe I have an idea for that as well, and one that will ensure Mr. Bingley remains behind." Lizzy grinned, pleased at the idea that had occurred to her. It could only bolster the courtship between her sister and Bingley if they had a few days together without Mr. Darcy's frowning interference keeping warm feelings from rekindling.

"That would mean you will travel with Mr. Darcy alone?" Jane sounded shocked by the idea. "That would be impossible."

Lizzy laughed. "You forget, Jane, that we are technically married, at least by law. There is nothing improper about it, and I am confident Mr. Darcy would never behave in an ungentlemanly fashion." Even if he hadn't been the honorable sort, there was no way he would risk the ability to get their annulment by removing the proof they had never consummated the marriage. Not that Lizzy would have responded kindly to such attempts on his part anyway, she hastened to assure herself.

"I am not sure this will work, Lizzy," Jane said a few minutes later after Lizzy had divulged her plan.

Lizzy pushed away any hint of uncertainty or lack of confidence. "Trust me. It will be a brilliant plan."

Chapter Three

Fitzwilliam hadn't realized it was possible to hurt quite so much and in so many places all at the same time. They'd only been at this work for half a day, but he was already sore and aching. His hands felt like they had been pulling weeds for hours, and he wondered if Lizzy had deliberately assigned him a job that would be utterly exhausting. Yet she and Bingley toiled nearby, so it didn't seem to be as though she had singled him out for one of the worst duties on the farm.

His gaze moved to Bingley, who was still talking quietly to Miss Jane Bennet, as he had done since almost the moment they had been reunited. Even while working at such a menial, laborious task, he seemed perfectly capable of conversation, and the two of them were laughing quite frequently.

His gaze darted to Fanny Bennet, who was looking fondly at the two of them from the chair where she sat with a glass beside her, and a parasol shielding her from the sun. Perhaps she was seeing all her scheming come to fruition, which set Fitzwilliam's teeth on edge. If Miss Jane succeeded in catching Bingley's attention again, he would likely marry her and return with her to England.

No doubt, Fanny Bennet was imagining she would come along, settling herself into the newlyweds' life and ingratiating herself into the Bingleys' and the Darcys' social sphere. He could hardly bear the thought of looking across the drawing room and having to see Fanny Bennet carrying on in her foolish ways, and he shuddered at the thought.

Finally, they heard the sound of a dinner bell ringing and soon trudged to the house. Mrs. Tucker had spread out food for all of them, and Fitzwilliam was starving in a way he'd never experienced before, but his hands ached so much that it was difficult to wield his knife and fork. He couldn't help glancing at Lizzy's graceful hands as she cut her food with effortless ease, as though the morning's work hadn't been nearly as exhausting for her.

She must likely be used to it, and while it should have made him think less of her that she could so easily step into a laborer's role, he found himself oddly admiring instead. This new life she lived was quite a change from what she'd had at Longbourn, but she seemed to have adapted with ease and perhaps even contentment.

He could not imagine living in such a fashion for long, but that she not only survived but thrived here indicated she was far more adaptable than he'd imagined. Could it be that she could hold her own in any London drawing room? Where he'd once seen her as wanting in many ways, now he wondered if perhaps he'd underestimated her abilities to grow and change.

It was a strange, pensive thought that had no place in his mind. He shouldn't care about her adaptability or anything else. Once the annulment was in place, he could return to England and find a suitable bride. It was time to fill the Darcy nursery, so he would look for a biddable young woman who would serve as a social asset but fade into the background of his life. He had no interest in falling in love or having the kind of happy marriage his parents had enjoyed. That was fine for Georgiana, but it didn't appeal to Fitzwilliam at all.

"I have had Mrs. Tucker working this morning to ensure you have food for the trip, Lizzy. Jacob had one of the farmhands looked over the wagon you will be using and ensure the horses are in good shape."

Lizzy seemed pleased by Kitty's words. "Thank you, dear sister, and you as well, brother." She smiled at Jacob as she said that. Though there was nothing at all intimate in the look, it still sent a tug of discomfort through Fitzwilliam to see her interacting so easily and openly with another man. He wouldn't label it jealousy, of course, for that implied a level of caring he didn't possess.

"What time will you leave?" asked Jane.

"Probably shortly after sunrise, unless that is too early for Mr. Darcy," said Lizzy with a pleasant smile, though there was clear challenge in her gaze.

He frowned at her. "I am quite accustomed to rising early."

"Yes, in direct contrast to most of the *Ton*, for we often stay out late and sleep late. I am shamelessly a lay-about," said Bingley with a charming grin.

"I am certain you are quite capable of working hard when the occasion demands it. You have demonstrated that very thing this day, Mr. Bingley," said Miss Jane with clear and open sincerity. She seemed to admire his ability to weed a garden as easily as he danced a quadrille.

Bingley flushed under her praise. "As always, I believe you give me too much credit, Miss Jane."

"It is a good thing you are quite adept at the task, Mr. Bingley," said Lizzy suddenly. "There are a great many acres to which we must attend, so Jacob can scarcely afford to lose an able body for the next few days while Mr. Darcy and I go to Cincinnati. It will be a big help to him if you are here to step into my place."

Mr. Bingley looked startled for a moment. "I had imagined I was traveling on with you to Cincinnati."

Lizzy frowned. "Oh, dear. I apologize if I misunderstood or assumed something. Of course, I am certain everyone can get by without me for a few days. It is not likely to impact the crops too much." She sounded doubtful as she said that.

Mr. Bingley frowned before looking at Jane and then back at Lizzy. "I do not see why I cannot step in for you, Miss Bennet. It would be an honor."

Fitzwilliam gritted his teeth, irritated that Bingley planned to stay behind, and it was clear Jane did as well. Obviously, this was some machination of Lizzy's, or perhaps her mother's. He glared at her, though she gave him an innocent look in return. She appeared to be unaware of why he was irritated, but he suspected she was simply a good actress.

"It is settled then," said Lizzy with a smile.

Fitzwilliam frowned as he realized neither Miss Jane nor Bingley planned to come with them. "Who will act as chaperone, Miss Bennet?"

Lizzy looked at him with a frown. "Do we require a chaperone, Fitzwilliam?"

He gasped. "Of course, we do. We are traveling alone together. It is unseemly."

"Technically, we are married, so there is nothing unseemly about it. It is not as though either of us will behave in a dishonorable fashion, is it?" She arched her brow, her look practically daring him to make a move that was dishonorable.

As if he would risk the annulment to do so.

"Of course, Jacob can spare Mama. She is above such menial tasks as weeding or farm work. Mama much prefers to oversee the interior and Mrs. Tucker, along with occasionally sitting outside to watch over us, as she did today." There was clear sympathy in Lizzy's words. Obviously, she pitied the housekeeper for being stuck in the role of babysitting Fanny Bennet.

He immediately shook his head. "You are correct. We do not require a chaperone." He would rather dance along the lines of propriety than be forced to endure traveling to and from Cincinnati in a jostling, bumping wagon with Fanny Bennet for several days. The only advantage would be that she could not meddle between Bingley and Miss Jane, but Fitzwilliam was feeling more and more certain preventing the union was a lost cause.

It didn't stop him from taking Bingley aside after lunch though, before they returned to more toiling, and pulling him into a sitting room. It was the same one he had used while speaking with Lizzy yesterday. "You must be careful, Bingley."

His friend frowned. "What do you mean?" There was a hint of defensiveness in his tone.

"It seems obvious that Miss Jane plans to make a play for you again. She will be here with her mother, and you are at their mercy. I implore you to use common sense and logic. Do not be swayed by emotion."

Bingley frowned at him. "I know you once believed that Miss Jane's affections were not true, and you made a compelling argument. It was fully my choice to walk away then, but I have regretted it, Fitzwilliam, and I believe I might have acted in haste. I have considered it off and on throughout the years, and I still love Miss Jane. She appears to still care for me as well, and you might as well know now I plan to do everything in my power to win her back. I know you do not approve, but I find that matters less to me than winning Miss Jane's heart. I wish I had not been persuaded to leave her almost four years ago."

Fitzwilliam thought about arguing, but what was the point? There was a new resolve and determination about his friend he was unaccustomed to seeing. And as he thought back over the last few years, he realized Bingley had certainly changed after Netherfield. Before meeting Miss Jane, he had been capricious, often finding a new object of affection upon which to dote, at least for a few weeks.

The longest his admiration had ever lasted was an entire season, but it had passed without him making an offer for the girl's hand. Since Netherfield, he had been quiet and more subdued. He interacted with the ladies of the *Ton*, but there were none who seemed particularly special to him, even for a few weeks here and there.

Certainly, Bingley had made no attempt to marry since then, or even court a young lady, and Fitzwilliam had to reluctantly accept the emotions were true, at least on Bingley's side. If Miss Jane could truly come to love his friend, he would withdraw his objections, but he was still uncertain that she wasn't too greatly influenced by her mother and lacking true affection. "I have spoken my piece, and I hope you will keep it in mind and be certain of what you feel, and what she feels and shows."

Bingley nodded. "I shall be sensible, but I will not be suspicious."

Fitzwilliam sighed, but he nodded. He had no inclination to argue with his friend when it was obvious Bingley had made up his mind on the matter. Fitzwilliam could only hope he didn't live to regret it and end up in an unhappy marriage from which there would be no escape. For he was certain Bingley and Miss Jane would not have an annulment option like he was lucky enough to have.

For some reason, the idea of being annulled from Lizzy caused an odd pang in him, instigating his chest to constrict in a bewildering fashion. How absurd.

Chapter Four

It was early when they started their journey, and neither of them spoke much. That suited Lizzy just fine, because there wasn't much she wanted to say to him, or at least nothing that would set a polite tone for a harmonious journey. For the first couple of hours, they rode mostly in silence as the day wakened around them.

It was predominantly flat terrain, but there were hills and enough changes in the landscape that required careful attention to the rough-cut road ahead of them. It was a simple path someone had made years before, and the wagon seemed to have a special affinity for finding every rut in the road, which sent jarring jolts through each of them. The third time Lizzy's teeth clacked together, she glared at Mr. Darcy. "Perhaps I should drive the wagon. I do know the route better than you."

He frowned at her. "It is a road. How difficult can it be?"

"It is no worse than some of the roads in England, but I do know where most of the jolts, dips, and bumps are." She held out a hand, wondering if he would surrender the reins.

He shook his head in irritation. "You are a most peculiar woman, Miss Elizabeth. I am quite capable of handling the driving."

"I look forward to you someday displaying your proficiency at it," said Lizzy with a hint of tartness before subsiding back into silence. The sun was starting to beat down with more intensity, and the orange had faded from the sky. It was mostly pure sunlight now with nary a cloud, so Lizzy reached behind her for her parasol, opening it to shield her face from the sun. She noticed Darcy was squinting as they drove along, and a slight adjustment of the angle of her parasol provided him some shielding for his gaze as well.

He cast her glance of surprise and a nod of thanks. "Your solicitousness is most surprising, Miss Elizabeth."

"Do call me Lizzy, Fitzwilliam," she said with a hint of exasperation. "It is only sensible to ensure you can see the road ahead of us, for I do not wish to die for your lack of mastery at the reins." She kept her tone overly sweet, barely smothering a giggle when his jaw tightened, and he looked away again.

Silence fell once more, and it was probably another hour before he spoke. "Why did you decide to come to America with Kitty when she married?"

"I thought it would be an exciting adventure, and there was nothing keeping me in England."

He frowned. "What about our marriage?"

Lizzy snorted before she could think better of it. "That was hardly a reason to remain, and it never really entered my calculations."

That was true. At the time Kitty had met and married Jacob, Lizzy had been married to Fitzwilliam for several months, of course not having seen him in that entire time. She had become adapted to the state and had even survived and grown a thick skin to the humiliation. Gossip, at least in Meryton, had mostly died down, and her life had resumed its normality. It had been so mundane and normal that the prospect of traveling to America with her youngest sister had beckoned and appealed in a new way.

"I did not mean for the sake of our marriage, but for our annulment. You did not even send information on how to find you. Nor did you indicate to Mrs. Collins that she should tell me, and so she barely revealed a thing. The woman was most stubborn and insistent about maintaining your privacy even under the influence of Mr. Collins when I called at Longbourn as the three years passed."

Lizzy beamed with pride. She wasn't certain why Charlotte had been so determined to protect her, other than she had been privy to how angry and hurt Lizzy had been at being forced to marry Fitzwilliam under his assumption that she had planned it, followed by his desertion. Perhaps she had misguidedly thought Lizzy didn't want the annulment. Whatever her reasons, she was pleased by her friend's loyalty.

"Charlotte is a sweet woman, but I never told her not to tell you. I truly did not think much of it either way, Mr. Darcy." She had thought about sending him a letter briefly upon realizing the third anniversary of their union had passed several months ago, but she'd never followed through. There was always something to do, and her life on the farm was a priority over the vague and shadowy idea of finally shedding a husband she didn't want.

"I would wonder that you could so easily overlook the consequences of your actions and how they affect me, but I should not be at all surprised."

"No, you should not," said Lizzy with true anger. "You showed no regard for my feelings or standing, and you refused to listen to anything when I tried to defend myself against your accusations. So, I do not understand why you would be at all surprised to find thoughts of you did not enter into decisions I make for my life, and they never shall."

He turned to her, obviously prepared to launch into a diatribe. It was interrupted by the wheel of the wagon catching a deep rut, but this time, it didn't roll on through. Instead, there was a cracking sound as the axle broke, and the wagon listed to the right. Lizzy found herself pressed against Fitzwilliam as the wood finished splintering, leaving them at an awkward angle.

After a moment, the wagon tipped over the rest of the way, and they tumbled to the ground. He landed first, and she landed on top of him, thankful to have him breaking her fall. He let out a strange sound, and she couldn't deny a little dart of pleasure at having landed so firmly against his diaphragm that it pushed the air from his lungs for a moment. Not that she wished to hurt him, but she didn't mind if he experienced a little discomfort.

She quickly rolled off him upon realizing the inappropriateness of their pose regardless of their married state and got to her feet. She took a few steps back and watched him, ensuring he was going to get up before she turned her attention to the wagon.

Lizzy sighed in annoyance as she looked at the broken axle. "This is quite a time-consuming repair, at least without the resources on the farm. We are not going anywhere in this wagon, Mr. Darcy. I think perhaps our best option might be to take the horses from here."

She grunted in irritation at the idea as she suggested it, for Lizzy was no horsewoman. She'd never felt comfortable in a saddle, and the horses apparently recognized her discomfort. In turn, she made them uncomfortable, and neither she nor the horse ever ended up enjoying it when she had to ride one.

He frowned. "There is but one saddle, Miss Bennet, and it is not a sidesaddle."

She shrugged. "I suppose I shall have to ride astride then." She'd gotten more comfortable with riding since moving to America, but it was never something she was going to enjoy, and her horse companion usually felt the same way.

She eyed the sorrel mare and the white stallion that had been pulling the wagon. They both seemed unharmed, and though she didn't know their names, she'd seen both before. She started to unhitch them, and she was surprised when Fitzwilliam stepped in front of her. "What are you doing?"

"That is hardly a lady's job."

Lizzy laughed. "There are not as many opportunities for the luxury of deciding what is and is not ladies' work living in Ohio, Mr. Darcy. Work is work, and it has to be done regardless of one's gender."

He frowned, clearly disliking that. "I am capable of this task."

She stepped back, half-hoping he wasn't, but he quickly figured out how to unhitch the horses, and he put the saddle on the stallion. Then he turned to Lizzy. "I thought perhaps you could ride with me, and we could use the mare to carry our things?"

Lizzy wasn't exactly thrilled with the idea, but it certainly sounded unappealing to ride bareback with no sidesaddle or any saddle at all when she wasn't very fond of riding as it were. "I suppose that would be a sensible idea," she said with real reluctance as she turned to the wagon. Between the two of them, they soon had several of the items they had packed tied to the mare's back, though they had to leave behind some of the food and all but two of the handmade quilts Mrs. Tucker had sewn.

Lizzy felt an uncomfortable sensation dart through her, one that made it difficult to breathe, as Fitzwilliam lifted her by the hips and placed her on the saddle moments later. There was certainly nothing dignified about her position as she spent a moment arranging her skirts to provide some protection between her and the friction of the saddle before he mounted behind her.

Having his arms around her as she leaned back against him caused another unsettling sensation. It certainly wasn't fear, but nor was it anything clear-cut like disgust or irritation. There was still far too much attraction between them, though she thought perhaps it might be on all on her side these days. On the other hand, he had been the one to kiss her first, so at one point in time, there had been a strong allure despite their unwillingness to acknowledge it. She tried to push that thought from her mind as they set out, with Lizzy determinedly ignoring any reaction she had to Fitzwilliam's arms around her.

WHEN THEY STOPPED FOR the night, it wasn't quite twilight yet. Lizzy wanted plenty of time to prepare a camp, and she was almost surprised Fitzwilliam wasn't grumbling about having to stop and sleep out under the stars. "You seem to be taking this better than I expected." She was unpacking food as she spoke.

He sat on the blanket beside her after having tended to the horses. "What do you mean?"

"I mean losing the wagon and having to ride together, not to mention having to stop and sleep outside. You surprise me, for you are most certainly out of your element, Mr. Darcy."

"I pride myself on being adaptable, Lizzy."

She had used his last name wondering what kind of response she'd get from him, but he seemed determined to ignore the way she was slipping in between his first and last name. Perhaps he was deciding to rise above any needling she did. That was an annoying thought for her, but she supposed it would certainly make for a more peaceful journey if they weren't constantly trying to provoke each other.

"I have spent quite a few nights sleeping out on this trip. I assume you traveled by flatboat to reach here?"

Lizzy nodded her confirmation, recalling the oftentimes unpleasant journey down the flat-decked boats, and sleeping outside underneath the stars. She couldn't help a small smile as she recalled her father's exasperation when he, Lydia, and Mrs. Bennet had finally reached the Middlemeer farm. He hadn't been annoyed about having to sleep out, but rather, having to hear Fanny complain about it each night for the entire trip.

He had never been so thankful for a bed, and it had all been on his wife's behalf so he could finally get a quiet night's sleep. He had been happy to share that with the entire table more than once during the weeks he'd been robust and in good health, before he'd fallen unexpectedly ill and passed away.

"Are you all right, Lizzy?"

She blinked, surprised by the tenderness in his tone. "I am fine. I was just recalling a memory of my father, who liked to complain about the way my mother had complained about the trip. It is quite arduous, and you must have been intent on getting this annulment. Is there a special woman back in England waiting for you to become free again so that you might make her Mrs. Darcy? Perhaps Miss Bingley?" She wasn't certain if she was teasing, genuinely pumping for information, or still trying to rile him.

He frowned. "There is not. It might suit you to remain in this limbo of a marriage, but it most certainly does not suit me."

Lizzy shrugged. "I confess it is convenient in some ways, for it dissuades the suitors in whom I have no interest. Being married is a rather distant thought for me, and it does not overly affect my life either way."

"It affects mine, I assure you." He was frowning at her. "It is time to fill the Darcy nursery and leave a legacy, but even if it were not, and I were content to allow Georgiana's heirs to inherit Pemberley, I could never bear to allow you and your mother to get away with the scheming you undertook at my expense."

Lizzy's breath hissed through her teeth at the suddenness of the vicious attack. "How dare you, Mr. Darcy? I do not know how many times I must tell you that I had nothing to do with our being compromised. You were so quick to cast blame and assume I conspired with my mother to make it happen, but you always seem to conveniently forget the fact that you kissed me first."

He scowled. "I..." It was obvious he planned to deny it, but perhaps he couldn't in good conscience, for he must surely remember he had been the one to initiate the kiss.

Not that she hadn't responded. Lizzy cleared her throat slightly. "I did not plan to trap you. I had zero interest in doing so, I assure you."

"Because you most certainly would have preferred Mr. Collins's limited prospects to mine," he said in a mocking tone.

She glared at him. "I had no intention of accepting Mr. Collins's proposal if he had gotten around to issuing one. I was happy to remain unmarried, and I would have embraced the title of spinster. I did not want you then, and I do not want you now, Mr. Darcy."

He got to his feet, ignoring the food remaining in front of them. "That suits me as well, Miss Bennet, for I still do not want you either. This marriage can be dissolved only too quickly for my taste."

"Then we are agreed on something." She turned her back on him, eating what remained on her plate through sheer determination. Her appetite had abandoned her in the face of their argument, but she had no desire to reveal that to him. He didn't need to see any of her weaknesses, and he certainly didn't need to know that his words had wounded her, despite her best efforts to harden her heart against him.

She cared perhaps more than she should for Mr. Darcy, but she was far too sensible to allow that treacherous bit of longing in her heart to derail her from her determination to be free of him. She certainly wasn't going to do something to humiliate herself, like admit that maybe trying to make their marriage work wouldn't be the worst idea in the world.

Considering it most certainly would, it was a foolish thought, and she quickly banished it before spreading out a bedroll near the fire and going to sleep, or at least trying. She feigned for a while before she actually managed to slumber, still seething with resentment at his accusations and the angry words they had exchanged.

Chapter Five

Fitzwilliam had spent some time stewing in angry silence, so he had fallen asleep later than he wished. Despite that, he was instantly awake at a furtive sound, because something about it made his hackles rise instinctively.

He sat up quickly and got to his feet, moving in a crouch to approach Lizzy. The dampened fire had burned nearly to coals, though there was enough illumination from the moonlight to see she was fast asleep. He heard another scraping sound, so he reached out and shook her shoulder briskly.

Her eyes popped open, and he put his hand over her mouth to keep her from crying out and warning whoever might be surrounding them in the darkness that they were aware of their presence. Her eyes widened, and then she started to look angry. He put his other hand to his lips, making a shushing motion before pulling away his hand. Before she could say anything, he bent closely enough to whisper, "I think there is someone surrounding us in the darkness."

Her eyes widened again, and she lost all sense of irritation, or at least it was no longer reflected in her expression. She hastily sat up, and he helped her to her feet. She grabbed a bag and stuffed in some random clothes before he dragged her to her feet.

"Leave all that." Fitzwilliam wanted to put her behind him, to offer her an extra level of protection, but he wasn't certain from which angle they were being attacked. Perhaps he'd just imagined it, since he wasn't accustomed to sleeping outdoors like this, but he didn't think he had. All the training he'd had at *Gentleman Jackson's* over the years didn't prepare him for the situation when he couldn't tell from where the danger originated.

"Are you sure?" asked Lizzy in a whisper/hiss, clutching the valise to her chest.

He nodded, though he was starting to doubt himself. When he was on the verge of admitting perhaps he'd made a mistake, there was a rush of feet as they approached, and with the level of aggression displayed, he was certain they weren't stopping by to check the status of their campfire.

At least they could now determine from which direction sounds had originated, and he jerked his head to the left, indicating Lizzy should go that way. She had time to grab a bag, and he did the same, but there was no time to salvage their knives or any other weapons, let alone bring the horses.

As they started to run, someone lit a torch behind them. Fitzwilliam was aware of the light, but he didn't pause or turn around to see who was attacking.

"They are getting away," yelled a male voice behind them, followed by a chorus of protests.

They had no light except for the moon to guide them, and it wouldn't have been safe to use one anyway. It would have led the attackers right to them. "Run faster." As he said that, he caught up with Lizzy, putting his arm around her waist and urging her to speed up. She somehow managed to despite the fact they were already running quickly, and he prayed neither of them would trip over an obstacle in the dark.

As though the thought had caused the action, Fitzwilliam grunted when his toe caught on a stray root, sending him flying forward to land on his palms and knees. He heard Lizzy cry out behind him, but then she was beside him, urging him to his feet. He still felt somewhat scattered, but they didn't have the luxury of him taking time to reorient himself. Instead, he got to his feet, and they continued running.

Fortunately, neither of them tripped again after that, and they ran into the darkness until they could no longer hear feet pursuing them. Fitzwilliam had been concerned that whoever was attacking had more interest in acquiring Lizzy than their supplies and horses, but perhaps that was an unfounded fear. Still, he wasn't about to let down his guard, though he noticed Lizzy was slowing.

Feeling slightly impatient, he turned to her. "I understand you are tired, but we must maintain a brisk pace until we are certain we are safe."

"Of course." There was a slight hitch in her breathing though, and as she started to move forward at a quicker pace, he saw her wince.

Fitzwilliam stopped, weighing the risk of doing so versus the need to know what was wrong with Lizzy. "Are you injured?"

"I am certain I shall be fine." Her repressive reply didn't encourage further inquiries as to her state of health, but there was suppressed pain in her tone.

With another sigh of impatience, he pulled her closer and turned so that the moon was fully illuminating her. He gasped at the arrow sticking out of her side. "How long has that been there?"

"I suppose since about the time you fell. When I paused to help you, one of them shot me." She looked pale, and her voice was thready. "I shall be fine, and as you point out, we must continue, Fitzwilliam. They might not yet have given up their pursuit."

She was repeating his words, and they were no less valid than they had been, but how could he expect her to push forward when she had an arrow in her side? "We can afford to slow down a little." It seemed to be the best solution to the problem.

She squared her shoulders. "We shall not make accommodations on my account, for I hardly feel a thing."

He thought she was putting on a brave front, and he hoped she was. Indeed, if she barely felt anything, that seemed more worrisome than if she was in great pain, considering the location of the arrow.

He put his arm around her waist to offer support. He could tell then just how injured she was, because she only glared at him slightly, and she made no move to push him away. Instead, she leaned her weight against him, allowing him to help her move along. He tried to take the bag from her once, but she tightened her hand around it and glared at him.

As they continued walking through the forest, no longer able to maintain a fast pace, his concern for her grew. Even with his help, she seemed to be slowing significantly, and he was hoping they could make it until sunrise. Then he might have a chance to see her wound and perhaps do something to care for it, though he had little training in such matters. He'd never served in the militia and had certainly never sullied his hands to train as a physician, let alone a surgeon. Now, he wished he'd undertaken such training, though managing Pemberley was quite a career in itself.

Finally, the first wisps of dawn started to fill the sky, and the gray around them lightened gradually as they could see the sun peeking over the horizon. When he got his first look at her in pale daylight, Fitzwilliam flinched.

Lizzy was practically ashen, and how she still managed to move shocked him. When he stopped for a moment, he released his hold on her. He simply wanted to see if she could keep herself upright, and she swayed before starting to collapse. He surged forward and caught her in his arms, lifting her and ignoring her protests as he held her against him. The valise she'd insisted on bringing was an uncomfortable lump between them, but he didn't request she discard it. "You are quite a bit more injured than you seemed, Lizzy." He couldn't help the note of censure that bled through his tone. "Why did you not tell me earlier?"

"It was not safe to stop, and I was not certain you would care anyway. Being a widower would be a cheaper and easier process than getting an annulment." It was difficult to tell if she was attempting humor, or if she genuinely felt that way.

He flinched. "I would not see you dead, even for all the freedom such a position would offer me. Would you wish me to be dead, Elizabeth?"

Her instant answer of, "No," was gratifying, at least. She might have little use for him, but she didn't want him deceased. How comforting.

"You cannot carry me. You must be exhausted after the night we have spent, so you should put me down. This is quite improper."

He rolled his eyes. "It was quite improper to travel together alone, but you assured me it would not matter since we are technically married. I submit that a husband can rightfully carry his wife, especially when she is in such an injured state, without raising eyebrows."

"Nevertheless, you must put me down." She sounded stronger than she had a few minutes ago, but she was clearly in no state to back up her demand with action. She was still in his arms, and despite her insistent words, she had curved against him and seemed quite content.

Surprisingly enough for him, Fitzwilliam realized he was content to have her there. Of course, she was an unaccustomed burden, but he found it quite tolerable to manage, and he couldn't deny there was a surge of protectiveness filling him as he contemplated her current state of health.

How much worse was she since he had allowed her to walk most of the night? Not only had he allowed it, he'd encouraged her to go faster when she started lagging behind before discovering her injury. A wave of guilt washed over him, and his arms tightened slightly around her. "You are fine as you are for now. We will stop and rest when I must."

"You are an insufferable man, who is always determined to control everything." She sounded grumpy, but she still wasn't fighting to get down.

He normally would have offered a sharp retort, but there was little to be gained by doing so. He suspected she was needling him in an attempt to distract herself from the pain, and since he was happy enough to carry her, he allowed silence to fall between them. That seemed to disgruntle her slightly, but she made no move to continue arguing or to make peace. She maintained silence as well.

He walked for at least another hour, though his muscles were starting to scream in protest. He was a relatively fit man, but carrying someone else took a toll, especially after the night they'd had. He was looking for a place he could set her down, perhaps on a fallen log, so he could rest for a bit and check her wound, when they heard horses ahead of them.

Fitzwilliam froze, jerking in the direction he heard it. Carefully, he lowered Lizzy to her feet and leaned her against a tree. "Can you stand here?"

She was grimacing, but she nodded. He wasn't confident she really could, but he saw no alternative. He put his fingers to his lips and waited until she nodded before he started to move away. He wanted to see who was approaching them, for he feared the villains who'd attacked their camp last night had somehow circled around them.

Before he had gotten far, the branches parted as a horse appeared in front of him. It bore a tall, large man on it, and there were two more horses tied behind the one with the saddle. The horses were laden with fur, and judging from the man's beaver hat, Darcy speculated he might be one of the French trappers who'd immigrated to the area.

The man seemed to confirm it when he drew up his horse with a sharp command issued in French. He stared down at Fitzwilliam for a moment, hand resting near his revolver, but he didn't reach for it. "Who are you, *monsieur*, and why are you in the forest?"

Fitzwilliam couldn't really explain why, but he started to relax marginally. He doubted this man had anything to do with attacking them. For one thing, those thieves had all appeared to be on foot, and even though they had likely stolen the horses Lizzy and Darcy had been riding, surely he and Lizzy would have heard them if they'd managed to circle around them through the forest and set up an ambush.

"My wife and I were attacked last night." It felt odd to identify Lizzy as such, for she truly didn't feel like his wife at all. He felt an instant of dissatisfaction at the thought, but he quickly pushed it away. "She is injured."

The man frowned as he got off his horse. He still appeared wary, and he didn't turn his back on Fitzwilliam, but he said, "Show me."

Fitzwilliam was wary about turning his back on the man, but what choice did he have? Aware of the man being able to grab his revolver and point it at Fitzwilliam at any moment, knowing he might feel a ball lodge into his back, he still turned and walked toward Lizzy as quickly as he could. He wasn't certain he was making the right choice, particularly by revealing her location, but he was out of options. If this man could help, he had to take the risk. If not, he would have to be prepared to defend her to the best of his abilities even without a weapon.

Lizzy was now seated on the ground. Clearly, she's been unable to maintain her balance or support herself enough to stay on her feet. He rushed to kneel beside her, taking her into his arms. His aching muscles screamed in protest, but he ignored the pain as he lifted her and turned to face the man who'd appeared on the horse. "Can you help her?"

"Perhaps." He frowned. "I believe my wife would be a better choice. She has some knowledge in healing. Our homestead is less than an hour away if your wife can handle being on horseback?"

"She has endured me carrying her this far, so I imagine the horse cannot be that much worse."

"Then come with me, *monsieur*."

"I am Fitzwilliam Darcy, and this is Elizabeth..." He almost added Bennet, but that would open the conversation to all sorts of awkward questions he didn't want to answer at the moment.

"I am Françoise Napier. I will take you to Rebecca, and if your wife can be helped, she is the one to do it." He sounded confident in his wife's abilities.

Fitzwilliam would have to find confidence in that, for he knew little about how to help Lizzy otherwise. For a man who was always in control and certain of his actions, it was a paralyzing feeling to be so helpless, and he loathed it entirely.

AFTER FRANÇOISE HAD moved all his fur to one of the horses and tied on Lizzy's bag as well, Fitzwilliam had mounted before Françoise handed Lizzy up to him. It was uncomfortable to ride bareback, but his discomfort was not his primary concern. Instead, he tried to keep Lizzy from feeling every jolt and rut in the road as the horse trotted along, but he supposed maybe it did not matter, for she'd lost consciousness a good forty-five minutes before.

He was frantic with worry by the time Françoise led them through the forest and into a cleared section. He could see a small log cabin before them, surrounded by corrals. There were a few horses, a couple of cows, and a goat. Smoke was coming from the chimney, and he was certain this must be Françoise's homestead.

"We are here," said the other man as he led them directly to the front of the cabin, dismounting his saddle and tying the horse to the hitching post there before coming over to Fitzwilliam and holding up his arms. It was difficult for Fitzwilliam to release Lizzy into the other man's embrace, because he didn't want to be away from her. It struck him as an odd thought, and the degree of his concern also seemed excessive for a woman he wanted to not be married to as quickly as possible.

He handed her down before sliding off the horse himself. He'd just taken Lizzy back when the door opened, and a petite woman stepped out. She had silky black hair, coppery skin, and she appeared to have at least some native lineage. "Françoise?" She spoke without an audible French accent, but there was some accent to her words. "Whatever is going on?"

"I found these folks in distress. They were set upon by thieves last night, and Mrs. Darcy has been injured."

Fitzwilliam went slightly stiff at the sound of the name, while imagining how much Lizzy would hate hearing herself addressed that way. It was strange and unfamiliar, but it wasn't entirely unwelcome to hear the name or think of her that way. For the briefest moment, he wondered if he was making the right decision with his insistence on proceeding with the annulment, but he quickly shoved aside the thought. It was not something to focus on now, for Lizzy's survival was paramount.

She waved him forward. "Come in immediately." She hurried in, and Fitzwilliam followed behind her with Françoise bringing up the rear of the procession. He laid Lizzy on a small bed near the fireplace at Rebecca's direction.

"This is our daughters' bed," said Françoise, who had clearly decided he would remain on the fringes. Fitzwilliam supposed he should join the man and give Rebecca room to work, but part of him couldn't manage to leave Lizzy. Fortunately, Rebecca didn't ask him to. Instead, she directed Fitzwilliam to start removing Lizzy's garments.

"I shall be outside," said Françoise abruptly. "Feel free to join me when you are no longer needed in here, Mr. Darcy."

Fitzwilliam nodded his agreement, blushing slightly as he started to undo the buttons on the back of Lizzy's dress. It wasn't the first time he'd entertained the idea of what she might look like without her clothes, but it was certainly the first time he'd touched her in such a way. Even though it was under these circumstances, it was still nerve-racking and a little embarrassing. He strove to hide that reaction, not wanting Mrs. Napier to wonder why he had not undressed his wife before.

He managed to divorce his thoughts from his actions, and he soon had her dress unbuttoned and removed to her waist. She had on a shift and corset underneath, and Rebecca surprised him by using a knife to cut through the shift after she had him undo the stays on her light corset to slide it off.

His breath hissed between his teeth when the wound was revealed, and he had to look away as Rebecca grasped the arrow in both hands and firmly broke it before tossing the end piece into the fire.

"Hand me the whiskey," said the woman.

Fitzwilliam frowned, thinking it was a poor time to drink, but he still reached for the bottle she indicated. It appeared to be homebrewed, and he realized her intention just before she uncapped it and poured it over the wound.

For a moment, Lizzy's eyes opened, and she screamed from the pain of it.

"Mama?" asked a small voice.

Fitzwilliam looked over, realizing then they had an audience. Two little girls, perhaps five and three, peeked at them from across the room. They still wore nightgowns, and their feet were bare. The older one was clearly concerned.

"It is all right, Adeline," said Rebecca briskly. "I am helping this woman. Will you help Jeannie dress and go to your papa?"

"Yes, Mama." With those small words, the little girl took the even littler girl by the hand and led her out of the room.

"She is out again." Rebecca sounded relieved by that.

"I am worried that she is not maintaining consciousness."

The other woman nodded, but she didn't look away from Lizzy and used her knife to start cutting gently around where the head of arrow had lodged in Lizzy's flesh.

Feeling weak, Fitzwilliam found he couldn't watch, though he could still hear the unpleasant process as the woman extracted the arrow. "Will she wake up?"

"It is early to say, but most likely. I am relieved she is unconscious for this part, but I have hopes that she will recover her senses once the pain has stilled, and she has a chance to rest. I believe your wife lost a lot of blood, Mr. Darcy."

He nodded, still not looking at the process. "I believe so as well. She hid the injury to start with."

"Ah, she did not wish to worry you. She sounds like a good wife."

Fitzwilliam opened his lips to protest, but then he realized he had no true objection to offer. They certainly had not lived as man and wife for any length of time, so he had no way to evaluate her worthiness or skill as a wife. He knew she was quite adept at scheming, particularly in conjunction with her mother, but he pushed aside the bitter thought before it could fully form. Now was hardly the time to nurture his previous resentments against Lizzy, particularly if she might not survive. He just nodded instead.

After a truly horrific few minutes filled with sounds Fitzwilliam was certain he would never forget, including a couple of deep groans from Lizzy despite her not fully and truly regaining consciousness, Rebecca finally stood up. "That is all I can do for now, Mr. Darcy. I will check her periodically, and I have some herbs to gather that will help with the pain and speed the healing. There are others I can give her to help her replenish her blood supply and feel stronger faster. Now, we must simply wait."

He nodded his understanding, not moving away from the bedside. He was still on his knees on the hard floor, but it was the first time he was aware of the discomfort. He looked down at Lizzy, pushing the hair off her face. She was still far too pale, and she was sweating slightly. He dared hope that was because she was so close to the fireplace rather than because an infection was already setting in.

As he trailed his fingers across her forehead again, sweeping back all the loose hairs that had evaded him the first time, he found it soothing to touch her. Perhaps she found it comforting as well, because her harsh breathing started to even out, and she appeared to be sleeping rather than in an unconscious state within the next twenty minutes.

He knew there was nothing he could do but wait and see, and that was maddening. He hated being so impotent in the situation, and he wished he could make her better just by the force of his will. Instead, he would be forced to endure the torturous passage of time that seemed to be creeping so slowly.

HE MANAGED TO TEAR himself away for a while, feeling he needed to help their host to repay his hospitality. Françoise's small homestead didn't have nearly the scope of work as the Middlemeer farm, but there were enough activities to keep the two men engaged well into the afternoon, when they paused at Rebecca ringing the bell. "Dinner is ready," said Françoise.

Fitzwilliam was relieved, for his muscles were still aching. Part of it was from carrying Lizzy, but the other part of it was from the unaccustomed hard work he had undertaken here and at the Middlemeer farm, and his stomach was growling. He had a feeling even the simplest fare would taste like it had been cooked by the Prince Regent's French chef after the day spent toiling.

He was also anxious to check on Lizzy again, but he hadn't felt he could justify excusing himself while there was work remaining to be done. He followed Françoise into his house a few moments later after they paused to wash up at an outside pump, and he immediately went to Lizzy, bypassing the enticing smells coming from the table.

He knelt on the floor beside her, taking her hand without thought as her eyes fluttered open. "Lizzy, are you awake?"

She turned her head to look at him, and there was awareness in her gaze. "I am. Thanks to Mrs. Napier."

"Rebecca," said the woman from the table. She looked slightly harried, as though she'd been doing too many things at once, but she still sounded polite and gracious.

"I was quite concerned about you." He made the admission past the lump in his throat. It was difficult to be honest with her, for it opened him to a new set of vulnerabilities, but what kind of cold fiend would he be to pretend he didn't care about her wellbeing at all?

"Thank you. If you had not carried me and found the Napiers, I would not like to imagine what my chances of survival would have been." She seemed slightly stiff as she gave her thanks, and it clearly pained Lizzy to have to acknowledge he had assisted her in any way, but she was making the effort to do so.

He stared at her for a moment, their gazes locking. Relief filled him, along with a certain warmth and kindness he was unaccustomed to feeling, particularly with Elizabeth Bennet. He had the strangest compulsion to lean forward and press a kiss to her cheek, but he managed to stave off the impulse. Abruptly, he realized he was still holding her hand. He started to release it, but she did so first, as though she had the same awareness at the same time. He leaned back and cleared his throat. "Do you feel like eating?"

"Mrs. Napier...Rebecca," corrected Lizzy hastily, "Fed me some broth before she made everyone else's luncheon. I am quite content for the moment, but I do still feel tired."

"Then you should rest."

Lizzy nodded. "We must get to Cincinnati quickly."

He frowned. "There is hardly such a rush that you would need to push yourself, Lizzy. Take the time you need to recover. Our task in Cincinnati will still be waiting for us." He was slightly offended by her clear surprise of his understanding and insistence that she rest. Did she think him completely unfeeling? Did she imagine that he was so eager to be rid of her that he would hastily eject her from her recovery bed and force her to continue with their trip to Cincinnati?

He squirmed slightly as he realized perhaps she had good reason to think that of him. He'd made no effort to hide his eagerness to attain the annulment, or his irritation that her relocation to America had slowed their progress significantly. He softened his tone. "The most important thing is for you to recover without further injuring yourself."

She still looked faintly surprised and perhaps a little troubled, but she nodded. "Thank you." She sounded puzzled, but her eyes closed, and she turned her head away from him.

He didn't wait to see if she fell asleep before returning to the table and joining the family there. He took the chair Françoise indicated, finding himself seated near the little girls. They were staring at him with open fascination, and he spent the rest of lunch telling them all about himself and England when Adeline inquired why he talked so funnily. Throughout it all, his thoughts dwelled on Lizzy even as he managed to go through the motions of socializing with the family who had rescued them.

WHEN HE AND FRANÇOISE returned to the cabin that evening for the night, Fitzwilliam was certain he'd never been so tired in his life. Even washing up with the cold water coming out of the handpump provided little refreshment, but it perked him up a bit.

Life on the American frontier was entirely too difficult compared to the comfortable life he had at Pemberley, and he still couldn't imagine why anyone would want to live such a way when they could have the comforts of England, or even Boston. It was certainly no London, but compared to these wilds, it was a veritable mecca of civilization.

Of course, he was not so rude as to comment on that or wonder what had brought the Napiers to embrace such a lifestyle. He'd gleaned throughout the afternoon that Françoise was from France, coming to Canada as a trapper as Fitzwilliam had assumed. He had met Rebecca, a member of the Ojibwe tribe, and they had married. When they moved to Ohio to claim free land, she had started calling herself Rebecca.

They seemed quite content there, and despite the level of hard work that must be involved, Fitzwilliam found himself feeling slightly envious as he watched their interaction throughout dinner. It was clear there was deep love between the couple, and he wondered how it would be to love someone like that.

After dinner, he approached Lizzy's bed. He was surprised to find her awake, and Adeline was sitting beside her. The little girl was reading to her from an illustrated book, and though she was clearly struggling with some of the words, Lizzy gave every appearance of being glued to the story.

Mrs. Napier followed behind him. "It is time to prepare for bed, Adeline."

"Where will we sleep, Mama?" asked the little girl.

"I have made you and Jeannie a bed in our room on the floor."

Fitzwilliam started to apologize for displacing the child, but it was obvious from Adeline's reaction that she was excited to have the opportunity to sleep in her parents' room. Still, he shot an apologetic look to Rebecca. "I am sorry for the inconvenience, Mrs. Napier."

She waved a hand dismissively. "It is no true bother, though I fear the bed is not big enough for both of you. I have also prepared a pallet for you on the other side on the floor. I wish we could offer another bed for you, Mr. Darcy, but we cannot."

"I am certainly not going to complain about what is available to me. Lizzy and I both owe you a great deal for what you have done for us."

FITZWILLIAM SPENT THE next two days helping Françoise and watching over Lizzy from a distance. He felt awkward about getting too close to her now that she was more alert and awake more often. She seemed to be recovering well, and it was always in the back of his mind that the reason they were where they were was because he was so insistent on obtaining the annulment.

Not that she had protested, and she seemed equally happy to get one, but he couldn't help feeling guilt and perhaps some doubt, particularly as he watched her interact with the Napiers' girls. He found himself one afternoon wondering what it might be like to come upon Lizzy on one of the large beds at Pemberley, with several children around her as she read to them like she was doing for Adeline and Jeannie. In his mind, the children he pictured were all a blend of himself and Lizzy, with her curly hair, his dark eyes, and a harmonious melding of their best features.

Disconcerted by the thought, he quickly turned and walked out again, though they had been about to have lunch. He was aware of Françoise following him as he walked over to the handpump. He had just washed his hands, but he went through the motions of doing it again as his new friend stood nearby.

"I do not wish to overstep, Fitzwilliam..." Françoise trailed off, as though expecting Fitzwilliam to tell him not to.

Fitzwilliam grunted as he dried his hands on a bit of muslin that was hanging from the pump.

"You and Mrs. Darcy seem somewhat aloof with each other. Is all well between you?"

Fitzwilliam thought about giving Françoise a set-down for the audacity to ask, but he realized he wished to discuss it. Without Bingley nearby, Françoise would have to step in. "We are *en route* to Cincinnati to obtain an annulment. We were compromised and forced to marry several years ago, and enough time has passed now..." He shrugged. "That is why we are distant. We have never gotten close enough to be anything else."

Françoise looked troubled. "You seem quite drawn to her. The concern and care for her is real, and you seem conflicted. Are you certain annulment is the best path forward?"

Fitzwilliam didn't like the hint of doubt that was starting to creep up, so he quickly snapped, "Yes, I am certain. It is what Miss Bennet desires as well."

Françoise frowned. "She seems like a lovely woman. Perhaps it would be better to look forward instead of behind."

Fitzwilliam walked closer, steeling himself for returning to the dinner table, where he would be seated across from Lizzy. She had been up to joining them for at least the last day. "I cannot do that. She manipulated the situation to force the marriage in the first place."

Françoise frowned. "Surely, if that were true, she would be protesting the idea of ending the union. Has she indicated she wishes to remain married?"

"No," said Fitzwilliam quickly, realizing there was a note of outrage in his tone. "She has been quite eager for it."

"It does seem a strange reaction from a woman who you claim went to so much trouble to trap you to start with." Françoise patted him on the shoulder as he walked past. "It must be troubling and difficult to decipher the correct path forward, but you do not look at her like a man who wishes to be rid of her. Perhaps you must rethink your priorities, Fitzwilliam. That is all I will say on the matter." Without another word, Françoise returned to the cabin.

Fitzwilliam was tempted to turn and walk away, trying to bring order to his thoughts. Instead, his rumbling stomach reminded him it had been too long since breakfast, and he was certainly made of stern enough stuff to sit across the dining room table and engage with the woman who would be his ex-wife in a short amount of time.

Chapter Six

Lizzy ignored the twinge in her side as she helped Rebecca clear the table after dinner, while the men finished the last of the tasks waiting outside. Adeline and Jeannie ran underfoot, and Lizzy found it quite enchanting the way Adeline imitated her mother and seemed to want to help, though she was a little too small to be much assistance.

Jeannie was more interested in playing, and Lizzy had to stifle a laugh when Adeline said to her sister in a perfect imitation of an exasperated tone she'd heard Rebecca use more than once, "Do sit down and stop fluttering like a butterfly. There is work to be done, Jeannie. Do not be such a baby."

Lizzy heard a small laugh and looked up, meeting Rebecca's eyes. The two of them grinned at each other as they walked to the sink. "Are you certain you feel up to assisting, Lizzy?"

Lizzy nodded. "I can hardly stay in bed another day." Her side was aching, but she was certain it was the healing process. It would be discourteous to remain in bed while her hostess did all the work and looked after her when she could stand and dry a few dishes. "You are quite lucky. Your daughters are adorable, and Françoise seems like a good man."

"Yes, I am blessed. I had to leave my people when I met and married Françoise, but I have few regrets. I am quite happy with my little family." Rebecca touched her stomach as though in an unconscious gesture. "Perhaps we will have a little boy this time."

Lizzy smiled. "You are with child?"

Rebecca nodded, looking pleased. "I have only just confirmed it, for I felt the baby move. Françoise is thrilled, and he assures me another daughter would be most welcome. I would like to give him a son though. Surely, every man desires a son. Your Mr. Darcy must?"

Lizzy shrugged. "No doubt." She finished drying the plate with the cotton square and placed it in the cabinet.

"You have been married many years?"

Lizzy shrugged. "About four."

Rebecca frowned. "You must not get discouraged. Sometimes, it takes longer than others to be blessed with a child."

Lizzy blinked at Rebecca. "Oh, we haven't tried to have a child."

Rebecca looked confused. "I did not realize it was something one could try or not try. In my experience, it simply happens."

Lizzy flushed, realizing Rebecca was talking about an intimate topic. "We are not together in that way, Rebecca. We were forced to marry back in England, and he blames me for the situation that brought about a compromise. He was always blunt with his intention to seek an annulment, and I have no objection. It is only recently that we have been reunited, and for the sole purpose of seeing to the dissolution of our marriage. There is nothing between us."

Rebecca gave a decidedly unladylike snort. "He does not hover around you and look at you like a man who feels nothing. He was most concerned about you the day you arrived here."

Lizzy shifted as another pain shot through her side. "Of course. He is not an unfeeling monster, and he does have concern for me, but there will be no marriage or children for me with Fitzwilliam Darcy. I can guarantee you that."

Rebecca shook her head, but she didn't seem inclined to argue. "Perhaps fate will take an unexpected turn."

"Perhaps, but I find it woefully doubtful, dear friend."

THEY WILED AWAY THAT day and the next with chores around the homestead. Lizzy was feeling better, save for an almost constant ache in her side now. It was starting to itch, so she assumed it was healing, thus she made no mention of it while helping alter one of Adeline's hand-me-downs for Jeannie.

A fierce thunderclap boomed so hard it made the cabin shake. Seconds later, torrents of rain fell from the sky, and it was enough to make Lizzy and Rebecca both set aside their sewing and go to the nearest window.

"I hope Françoise and Mr. Darcy are all right," said Rebecca. "They were going to the higher pasture to check on the cows this morning."

"I thought you had just the two," said Lizzy.

Rebecca shook her head. "Those are the milk cows, but the ones in the pasture are mostly a food source, though some will be allowed to breed for next year's supply. I do hope they are not caught out in this."

"I am certain they will be all right." Lizzy said that in a bracing way, though she wasn't entirely certain at all. The rain was really coming down, and she could see how it might impede visibility. The thought of the men losing their way and becoming lost in such conditions chilled her, and she couldn't deny she was terribly concerned for Fitzwilliam.

As the afternoon progressed into evening with no sign of the men's return, Rebecca was clearly growing more and more fretful. Lizzy was as well, but she was doing her best to keep her new friend and her daughters as calm as possible.

"I must go look for them." Rebecca suddenly burst out with that announcement as she got to her feet. It was several hours later, and the rain was still coming down.

Lizzy shook her head. "It would be dangerous to go out there."

"They must be lost, or they could be injured. You will stay here with the girls, and I will go look for them, since I am more familiar with the land."

Lizzy frowned. "I do not think that is a good idea." She groaned as she got to her feet, noticing a sharp pain shoot through her side as she did so. "It will not serve any purpose if you get out there and come to be lost as well."

"You do not understand, Lizzy. Françoise is my life. I cannot bear to be without him. The idea of him being injured or..." She trailed off with a wail that she quickly stifled when Adeline and Jeannie looked up at her in concern. "I must look for him," she said again, more softly.

Lizzy wasn't certain how to dissuade her, so she couldn't express the relief she felt when the door opened moments later as Rebecca was donning a pelisse, clearly planning to go out into the rain against all common sense. Lizzy couldn't blame her, for part of her was compelled to as well, but she was certain her getting lost would just make the situation worse. She'd been trying to dissuade Rebecca, but the arrival of Françoise and Fitzwilliam did that well enough that she didn't have to worry about it.

Instead, she rushed to Fitzwilliam, realizing she was greeting him with a surge of relief to find him safe, though he was soaking wet. Unlike Rebecca, she managed to keep herself from throwing her arms around him and embracing him. "You look dreadful, Fitzwilliam."

He smiled, though his teeth were chattering. "It is rather wet and cold out there."

"I can well imagine." From the corner of her eye, she watched Rebecca lead Françoise into the bedroom, and the girls followed behind. Realizing Fitzwilliam was shivering with the cold, she pulled him to the fireplace. "You should start undressing."

She ignored the stretching sensation in her side as she knelt to retrieve their bags from under the bed. Fitzwilliam had a nightshirt in there, and it would have to do for the moment. She pulled it out for him and got to her feet, swaying slightly unsteadily as she gripped the banister of the footboard, waiting until she regained her balance before turning to him.

He was still struggling with the buttons, and she realized his hands were shaking so badly that he might not be able to manage them alone. It was a daunting task to imagine helping him such an intimate chore, but she moved closer and started unbuttoning his buttons. When he protested, she sent him a look of censure that silenced him, quickly stripping off his jacket, followed by his waistcoat, and his shirt.

She left him to deal with the pants, not quite that brave, before moving to the kitchen to get a piece of muslin for him from the stack Rebecca maintained for drying dishes. She returned and handed it to him, finding him bare from the waist up. She did her best not to look at him as she handed him the cloth and turned her head.

His teeth were still chattering slightly, but she heard a rustle of damp clothing, and she could imagine him drying himself with a towel. She'd seen enough to have a pretty good visualization of his body, and she was shocked at her mind conjuring an image of the cloth rubbing over his smooth flesh. It caused her to shift, which made a pain shoot through her side and distracted her, to her relief.

"I am decent now," he said a moment later.

She turned to face him, finding his hair was still wet, but he was in his nightshirt now, and only his calves and feet were bare. She nodded as she bent down to retrieve his clothes, bringing them close to the fire to hang on hooks arranged there. With luck, they would be dry by morning. "Rebecca was quite concerned about Françoise," said Lizzy softly, still not looking at him.

"With good reason. It was quite worrying. There was a brief point in time that I was afraid we would not make it back due to all the mud. Fortunately, Françoise knows his land well, and he navigated the way back with confidence."

"I was worried as well," said Lizzy, having to take a deep breath for courage before she made the admission. She looked at him slowly, gauging his reaction. "I did not like the idea of you not returning, Fitzwilliam."

His expression softened. "Believe me, I did not enjoy the prospect either, Lizzy."

She realized he was still shivering, and his hair was wet. She dragged him closer to the bed. "Get under the covers." He did so with a modicum of help, and she took the cloth from him, bringing it closer as she bent forward to dry his hair. It caused her side to stretch painfully, but she pushed down the pain as she dried his hair.

When she pulled back the cloth, she realized her arms were almost around him, and her hands were resting on his shoulders. She was hovering above him, and his head was tipped up. He started to tip it down, and she was certain he was about to kiss her. She had no objection to that, but the chattering excitement of Adeline and Jeannie returning to the room caused her to jerk away, breaking the moment.

She took the cloth and hung it by the fireplace as well before moving over to sit on the wooden seat that doubled as a couch. She did her best to avoid interacting on too personal of a level with Fitzwilliam for the rest of the evening, and the worsening pain in her side provided ample distraction.

She was able to push aside the worry she felt for him, along with the relief at having him safe, and all the doubts her feelings brought to her. Instead, she clung to the pain almost like a talisman, convincing herself it was simply because she was healing, and she was grateful to have it to focus on. Anything that distracted her from the confused feelings he inspired had to be a good thing, even if it caused pain.

Chapter Seven

After the exhausting ordeal of fighting their way back through the mud and heavy rain, Fitzwilliam fell asleep easily. He woke sometime in the middle of the night to realize the fire had gone out, and the room was cold. He was also in the bed Lizzy had been using, and he felt a wave of remorse that he hadn't woken up enough to leave it to give back to her. She was still recovering from her injury, and the last thing she needed to do was sleep on the floor.

He wondered what had woken him, but when he heard a moan, he realized the sound was familiar. With a frown, he slid out of bed and walked over to the fireplace, spending a moment relighting it before turning to Lizzy. The moan came again, and he grasped it was originating from where she laid on the pallet on the floor. He walked closer. "Lizzy?" He thought perhaps she was having a nightmare.

It was only as he got close enough to feel the heat coming off her that he realized it was far more than a nightmare. He pressed the back of his hand to her forehead and winced at the heat. She was feverish, and she was clearly thrashing about in the throes of it. He ignored the impropriety of doing so and started unbuttoning her nightgown.

She wasn't wearing a shift beneath it, since it had been cut by Rebecca to treat her wound, so he was able to immediately see her side. It was bandaged, so he started to pull off the cloth covering it. He hissed at the sight of angry red flesh, bending down and lifting her to place her in the bed before going to Françoise and Rebecca's room. He knocked on the door, and Françoise appeared less than a minute later.

"I am sorry to disturb you, but Lizzy is feverish. I think Rebecca needs to look at her."

"Of course." Françoise closed the door, and Fitzwilliam returned to Lizzy. He sat on the bed beside her, taking the opposite side so that Rebecca would have room to maneuver, and he took Lizzy's hand in his. "Stay with me, Lizzy." As he clutched her hand, dire thoughts filled his mind.

The idea of losing her was unbearable, and he realized he cared more for Lizzy than he'd ever planned. Was it enough to build a marriage while knowing she had been so deceptive to force them into it? He couldn't say but was certain his world would be far more detrimental without Lizzy in it as he waited for Rebecca and clung to the hope she would somehow pull Lizzy through this crisis.

She joined them shortly, fussing over Lizzy. He grew ill when she had to use her knife once more to release the infection that had been building. Lizzy thrashed through that, and he had to help hold her down. As he looked down at her, he wished he could take her pain as his own. His mouth acted without his brain's permission, sweeping forward to kiss her cheek. "You must fight, Lizzy," he whispered.

"She will," said Rebecca in a strong voice. "She is a fighter, Mr. Darcy. This is only a setback." She turned to her husband, who hovered uncertainly in the doorway of their room. "I need several herbs." She reeled them off for him before turning to Fitzwilliam. "You will boil cloths, Mr. Darcy. After the pus drains, I will need to bandage this again."

He nodded, happy to have something to contribute, though he half-suspected it was a mission of mercy she'd invented to give him something to do with his hands. He hovered nearby, doing whatever Rebecca asked as the hours passed.

Near dawn, when Lizzy's fever finally broke, and she appeared to be resting instead of unconscious, relief filled him. Once again, he wondered if he could get past how their marriage had come about to make the most of it and find a happy future with Lizzy. Was such a thing possible now that he knew he wasn't going to lose her?

Chapter Eight

Lizzy felt remarkably unscathed considering the experience as she and Fitzwilliam departed from the Napier family three days later. Fitzwilliam had purchased two horses from Françoise, but only after he had been sure Lizzy felt like traveling. She most certainly did, craving activity after having been confined to bed for so long.

The infection had taken quite a bit out of her, and she would always have a scar. That was partially from the arrow, but also from Rebecca having to cut around the infected area when she'd been so sick and drain the wound. Still, it was a minor inconvenience considering she was alive and well now, and she felt a dart of regret at having to part from the Napiers. They didn't live close enough for easy visits, but she and Rebecca had already planned for the Napier family to come to the Middlemeer farm in the fall, and then she would come back to visit them again next spring.

As they rode along, Fitzwilliam seemed to keep wanting to bring up something. He'd open his mouth, say her name, and then trail off into silence. It was quite maddening, and a little alarming too. She wasn't certain what he wanted to say, but she was fairly sure she didn't want to hear it.

He was probably going to tell her he was happy she was all right, but he was still resolved to get the annulment. After all, he still blamed her for forcing the situation even though he'd been the one to kiss her, and her mother had discovered them through no fault of Lizzy's. She couldn't convince him of that, and she didn't want to hear him confirm he still wanted to end their marriage. Lizzy knew it was a sensible decision, and if she did so, she might still find a man with whom she could be happy someday, but her heart cried out at the idea.

She had a sneaking suspicion that she might have started to care a great deal about Fitzwilliam in the time they had been with the Napiers. It certainly hadn't been her intention, so she wanted to put distance between them and end their business as quickly as possible before she did something utterly foolish, like completely fall in love with the man.

When he obviously wanted nothing to do with her, it would be imprudent to hand him her heart just for him to trample upon it. She was content to allow silence to reign between them, so she feigned tiredness for the rest of the ride.

Thankfully, they arrived in Cincinnati late that afternoon. He selected a hotel, seemingly at random, though it appeared to be a nice one. He stopped in front of it, tying the horses to the hitching post, and he took her arm after he helped her down. "I believe for safety's sake, it would be better if we shared a room, Lizzy."

She was torn about that, for propriety dictated under normal circumstances they would never share a room, but they were technically married. After the experience they had gone through, she wasn't entirely certain she wanted to be alone in a room of her own anyway. She felt much better than she had after she had fallen ill again from the infection, but she wasn't entirely confident that it was a good idea to be away from any help should she require it. "That is probably a sensible idea, Mr. Darcy."

He frowned. "Why are you calling me Mr. Darcy now?"

Lizzy blinked, not having realized she had done so. "I do not know. I suppose I fell back into the habit since we are now among more people again. Yes, I believe we should share a room, Fitzwilliam."

He nodded his agreement, and they entered the hotel lobby.

It was nice enough for the area, and there was a naked cherub statue in the middle of the floor, crafted from white marble. Lizzy grinned at a mother walking by, shielding the eyes of her boy, who could have been no more than eight. He had been avidly staring at the naked cherub, and the mother looked like she was about to have the vapors. Lizzy managed to hold off her laugh until the woman and boy had passed, and she giggled softly.

Fitzwilliam looked at her, but he didn't inquire as to the reason for her amusement, and she didn't bother to share. Instead, she stood beside him as they waited their turn in front of the reception desk. Her arm was still through his, though she knew was for propriety's sake, and he'd offered it out of politeness. Still, she couldn't deny part of her liked being so close to him, and having his skin so close to hers, separated by only a few layers of fabric.

She'd found herself maddeningly thinking of his skin far more since she had seen so much of it after the rainstorm. It was an unwanted distraction, because she couldn't seem to banish it from her head.

Finally, they approached the front desk, and Fitzwilliam arranged for them to have a room with two beds. As he was signing the register, he asked, "Is there a solicitor around?"

"You will find a few lawyers in town," said the young man manning the desk. "There is one just a couple blocks up and to the right. Look for Shamus Harry's office. He seems like a good enough lawyer."

"What makes you say that?" asked Lizzy.

The young man shrugged. "He has a nice sign."

Lizzy wasn't certain that inspired confidence, but she didn't argue with the young man. Instead, she and Fitzwilliam handed their bags to an eager young man waiting to take them to their room.

"Shall we find this Mr. Henry?" asked Fitzwilliam.

"Yes, but I think he said Harry."

Fitzwilliam nodded, pausing for a moment to tip the young man handling their bags before taking Lizzy's arm again.

They left the hotel at a sedate stroll after arranging for the hotel's livery service to board the horses for the night. Lizzy could pretend it was just a mundane trip, and that they were there simply to run a few errands, and perhaps buy some new clothes, which she desperately needed after losing all her supplies, save for the one bag, to those bandits. Yet, it needled the back of her mind that she was there to obtain a formal dissolution of her marriage to Fitzwilliam. That should make her happy instead of leaving her with a vague and aching trace of regret.

They found Mr. Harry's office easily enough, and he did have a nice sign. Whoever had done it had paid meticulous attention to detail and had clear experience with calligraphy. She wasn't certain that made him a qualified lawyer, but he seemed competent enough despite his young age as he greeted them.

He was certainly fast. He seated them, got a sense of what they wanted, and said, "Come back tomorrow afternoon, and I shall have papers ready for you to sign," in under ten minutes. He reached into his desk and removed a piece of paper and a pen. "I shall give you a list of the town's physicians, Mrs. Darcy, and they can confirm the current state for the courts." He flushed slightly as he said that, not looking up at her.

Lizzy inferred he was talking about the physical exam she had yet to undergo and would be forced to do so to prove there had been no consummation of the marriage. She writhed with embarrassment and not a little bit of resentment at the thought, but there was no way around it. "Thank you," she said through gritted teeth as she took the list from him a moment later.

"You do not have to see to that yet. I can have the paperwork arranged for you, but you will definitely need to include a letter from a physician before Mr. Darcy returns to England to file for the annulment, ma'am."

Lizzy nodded as she folded the paper and put it in her reticule. "Thank you." She wasn't quite as short with him this time. After all, it wasn't the young man's fault she was in the situation. She supposed it was no one's fault but her own for having allowed Mr. Darcy to kiss her all those years ago and lead them to a compromising position that her mother had so gleefully discovered and exploited.

After leaving the lawyer's office, they did a little shopping to replenish a few of their supplies, and then they returned to the hotel. When they reached the lobby, Fitzwilliam said, "You should go on up. There is something else to which I must still attend." He passed her a key.

Lizzy was slightly offended he wasn't seeing her to their room, but she realized that was a silly sentiment. He'd made no attempt to hide he was eager to be rid of her, and she was perfectly safe entering the hotel on her own and walking up a few flights of stairs. "Very well." Without another word to him, she took the key and entered the hotel. Lizzy stopped long enough to speak to the concierge, requesting a bath be sent to the room. She decided Mr. Darcy could afford that indulgence, since he had been the one to pay for the room, and she went upstairs.

After Lizzy's bath was the delivered, she sank into the hot water and put a cloth over her face as she indulged in a few tears. She couldn't entirely verbalize why she was crying, except perhaps she'd dared to hope more than she should have that Fitzwilliam might change his mind.

She hadn't even consciously realized she'd already changed her own mind about wanting an annulment. She'd been firmly convinced until they were seated before the attorney that it was her greatest wish as well, but it all crashed down upon her now. The reality of the situation, of her failure at the marriage, and her inability to get through to Fitzwilliam, seemed to catch up with her.

After she cried, she found herself feeling much better though, and she finished washing. She had just exited the tub and wrapped a cloth around herself when she heard a key turn in the lock. She let out a startled gasp, not having time to dart behind the dressing screen before Fitzwilliam entered.

She stared at him, paralyzed with horror or perhaps something else, as he entered. He stumbled to a stop while he stared at her openmouthed for a moment. "I apologize." He quickly averted his gaze and closed the door. "I did not realize you would be bathing."

"I did not realize you would be back so soon," said Lizzy with perhaps more tartness than she meant. "I assumed you would be quite a while with your mysterious errands."

He wasn't looking at her, but he came closer, holding out a bag. "I noticed a certain shop when we were getting clothes before, and I thought this might be handy for you. I know Mrs. Napier had to destroy the one you had with you to get to your wound."

Lizzy took the bag before darting behind the dressing screen. She wrapped the cloth around her and secured it so she would have a hand free before reaching into the bag. When she pulled it out, she blinked in stunned silence at the fine French silk she was holding in her hands. It was adorned with lace, and she quickly realized she was holding a new shift.

She had picked up a couple of dresses during their shopping, but she had been too embarrassed to buy underthings in front of him. He must have noticed, and she was mortified for a moment, and then she was intrigued as she realized he'd been paying that much attention to her purchases. She doubted it had been because he worried about pinching pennies, and a glow suffused her as she imagined him thinking about her without her underlayers, realizing she had lost her shift to the knife Rebecca had used to save her life. He must be thinking about her in a more than impersonal way.

Her hands trembled as she quickly dried off and slipped on the shift. It was as soft and fine as any garment she'd ever owned, and her eyes welled with another round of tears that she managed to successfully stave off.

"I thought you might like to have dinner in the hotel dining room?" asked Fitzwilliam from the other side of the screen.

"Yes, that would be delightful." Lizzy finished dressing, glad she had selected one prettier dress and one practical one for the return to Middlemeer farm. She rejoined Fitzwilliam a short time later, aware of him watching her every move as she pinned up her hair before adding a hat. It was also a new purchase, and she felt fun and adventurous as she pushed back from the vanity table and stood up. He offered his arm, and they departed the room together moments later.

He paused in the hallway to lock the door before turning back to her. There was a ruddy hue to his cheeks when he said, "You look lovely, Lizzy."

"Thank you, Fitzwilliam." She was aware of the fine silk and lace against her body, and it made her walk with a new awareness of her skin with each movement. She basked in the sensation, just as she basked in Fitzwilliam's attention over dinner. They spoke like friends, and perhaps more.

There was no mention of the annulment, and she found herself unexpectedly enjoying their time together. When the meal had ended, and it was time to return to the room, she felt a strange fluttering sensation in her stomach as she wondered if their new accord would spill over and last, or if they would be as strangers when they got back to the room.

He unlocked the door a few minutes later, indicating she should enter first. Lizzy slipped inside, and she hovered between the two beds as she stared at him for a moment. He was staring at her as well, and she wasn't certain if it was a mutual decision, or if it was a moment of madness when she considered it later, but the next thing she knew, she was walking toward him, and he was approaching her.

Fitzwilliam's arms went around her, and she wrapped hers around his neck. His mouth touched hers, at first gentle and hesitant, but soon deepening to a more intense passion. It reminded her of the night they had kissed the very first time, and for a moment, she indulged strictly in that recollection, along with the pleasure this moment brought her.

Inevitably, his anger afterward crept into her mind, and his certainty that she had been in cooperation with her mother to ensure they were compromised. That brought a dart of sanity, and she pulled away. "We cannot do this. It will ruin all chance of you having your annulment, Fitzwilliam."

His expression darkened slowly, and he took a step back. He cleared his throat and nodded. "My apologies. I do not know what came over me."

Lizzy managed a sharp nod as she turned away from him, feeling her heart squeezing in her chest. How she had hoped he would say something entirely different.

All her hopes had hung on the possibility that he might deny he still wanted the annulment. What a fool she had been. She needed to hear the assurance that he no longer wanted to set her aside, but all she had done was get confirmation. Even worse, she knew now she had fallen in love with Fitzwilliam despite the odds.

It was the most foolish thing she could have done, but she could see no way that she could have prevented the feelings from developing in light of the circumstances. She only hoped they could be transient and fleetingly shallow, soon departing as quickly as they came. With any luck, by the time Mr. Darcy was in Boston to catch a boat back to England, Lizzy would have forgotten all about this foolishness and the man himself.

As she returned to the dressing screen, awkwardly undoing the buttons before donning her sleeping gown, she found little optimism in the thought. She clung to the hope that she could forget all about Fitzwilliam Darcy, but she doubted it would be as simple as that. When the door shut behind him moments later, she winced at the sound and hung her head. Tears burned her eyes, but she refused to let them fall.

Chapter Nine

Fitzwilliam reared back from her as she disappeared behind the dressing screen. He didn't wait to speak to her again, turning away from her and exiting the room without a word. He wasn't certain what to say, but her reminder that the annulment was at stake with their imprudent actions had been like a dowsing of cold water in his face. It was a stark reminder that she still wanted to be free of him, and as he unthinkingly made his way downstairs, darting into the saloon that was attached to the hotel, he was forced to realize certain assumptions he'd held for so long were false.

If she was this determined to obtain an annulment, clearly she had not been conspiring with her mother to force him into the position of marrying her to start with. Had she been, she wouldn't have departed for America and made it difficult to find her. She would have stayed in England and tried to capitalize on her technical position as Mrs. Fitzwilliam Darcy. He had been a fool, utterly misjudging everything about her in his haste to assume the worst.

He shook his head as he took a seat at the bar, nodding his acceptance when the bartender suggested a whiskey. He tossed it back as he ruminated on the foolish choices he'd made. He had been so certain that Fanny Bennet's daughters were just like their mother, and he had felt a deep sense of betrayal when it seemed confirmed that Lizzy was cut from the same cloth.

He had been angry and lashed out, refusing to recognize that she had been caught up in it as well. Her words returned, reminding him he had been the one to kiss her first, but he always conveniently overlooked that fact, because it didn't fit the narrative he wanted to believe. It had been easier to blame Lizzy, to tell himself she had been a co-conspirator, than to recognize she had been a victim as well.

If he had done that, he might've been compelled to make a true effort to make their marriage work rather than just set her aside and force her to endure such humiliation. That hadn't been what he wanted, so he'd deliberately blinded himself to any reality but what he'd embraced.

Now, it was clearly too late. He had changed his mind. That was a blunt and stark fact that hung before him, one that was completely inescapable. After spending time with Lizzy, he no longer wanted to set her aside or obtain an annulment. He wanted to make their marriage real and lasting. Yet she clearly had no interest in doing so, or else the annulment wouldn't have been foremost in her mind. She wouldn't have had the ability to push him away and think clearly about their future goals if she had any interest in being his wife.

Thanks to his own actions, he had completely decimated any chance of winning over Lizzy. It was a thought that haunted him throughout the evening as he drank far too much and ended up in a card game, where he lost far too much money as well. Finally, in a somewhat drunken stupor, and many pounds lighter in his pockets, he stumbled from the saloon and back into the hotel.

As he walked up the stairs, some bit of logic returned, and he realized perhaps he should just tell her how he was feeling. Maybe he was misjudging the situation, and perhaps she would be amenable to the idea of trying to make their marriage work. Yes, the more he thought about it, and with the whiskey inflating his confidence, he decided it was a sound plan.

He would simply enter the room, tell her he'd changed his mind, and insist they stay married. She was bound to agree, was she not? He had himself entirely convinced of that by the time he reached the room.

He had to fumble to an embarrassing extent to get the key in the lock, but it finally yielded and turned, and he stepped inside the room.

It took him a moment to realize the room was dark, save for the light coming in through the lightweight curtains. Lizzy was in her bed, and it was obvious she was fast asleep. For a moment, he hovered over her, contemplating waking her. It was only when he recalled what she had been through, and how much she still needed her rest, that he managed to stay the impulse.

Instead, feeling defeated once more, he turned to his bed and collapsed upon it. He made no effort to undress or focus on personal tasks. His thoughts were too consumed with her and the realization that he had lost all chance of happiness with Lizzy Bennet.

Chapter Ten

Lizzy wrinkled her nose the next morning at the faint stench that remained in the room, quickly identifying the origin as Mr. Darcy's clothes. She thought of him as Mr. Darcy this morning, because he was cool and aloof, and he barely looked at her. Of course, he seemed to be having difficulty holding up his head, and his gaze was inordinately bloodshot. Judging from the foul odor of smoke and alcohol clinging to his clothes, he'd spent considerable time in the gentlemen's lounge the evening before.

Briefly, Lizzy wondered if she might have driven him to that point by the reminder that he wanted the annulment, but she quickly dismissed the thought. No doubt, he had been down there celebrating a return to sanity and his imminent freedom. Perhaps he'd even found a young woman of ill-repute to keep him company. The thought made her stomach burn with nausea, and she quickly shoved aside the notion.

She told herself it was no business of hers what company he kept as she dressed for the day before walking to his bed. Lizzy shook his shoulder firmly, feeling no sympathy when his eyes opened again. He'd looked at her earlier in the day with his bloodshot eyes, but at some point while she'd been dressing, he'd returned to sleep. She kept her voice steady, perhaps a shade louder than necessary, when she said, "You must freshen yourself, Fitzwilliam, for we are due to meet with the lawyer soon."

He groaned and rolled out of bed, causing that foul stench to accompany him. She wrinkled her nose and reared back, grimacing at him. "I will go down for breakfast. You can join me when you are ready."

He grumbled something, and she saw him moving toward the bath. She wondered if he planned to use the cold water, and she decided if he did, it was a punishment he deserved for his night of excesses. She could find no sympathy for him as she imagined him imbibing a prodigious amount of alcohol in celebration of his forthcoming liberty from her.

With another sniff in his direction, she grasped her reticule and exited the room. She walked down the stairs and entered the dining room, ignoring the slightly askance look from the young man standing there. Clearly, he believed she should have an escort. Normally, she would have, but she wanted to escape from Fitzwilliam, particularly since she suspected he was currently taking a cold bath.

She hoped he endured discomfort for every moment of it as she followed another young man to a seat. "I will have my husband join me shortly," she said to the young man as he started to hand her one menu. He nodded and placed another beside her before taking her order for a pot of tea.

She had not yet ordered breakfast when Fitzwilliam joined her a few minutes later. His eyes were still bloodshot, but his hair was restored, and his skin looked slightly pink, as though he'd scrubbed it with cold water. She hid a pleased smile behind her teacup as she had a sip. "You look ready to greet the day now, Mr. Darcy."

He surprised her by groaning softly. "I do not feel that way. Last night was a foolish mistake."

For a moment, her heart skipped a beat as she thought he might be referring to pulling back from her, though it was far more likely he was referring to the foolish mistake of kissing her to start with. "Oh?"

He nodded and winced. "I drank far too much. It was uncannily like being a youth back in the days of visiting my first gaming hell."

Lizzy frowned her disapproval. "Yes, I could see how that could be a mistake." She was saved from having to offer further conversation by the return of their server, who took their orders. She made no effort to engage Mr. Darcy in conversation, and he seemed content with his silence. It was a prolonged, uncomfortable breakfast that they endured, and it was a relief when they could finally step outside the hotel sometime later and walk back to the lawyer's office.

As they approached, Lizzy's stomach clenched with anxiety when she realized the moment was upon them. Once she signed the documents and submitted herself to the humiliation of an exam so Mr. Darcy could take proof that she remained pure to England, this chapter of her life would be over. She should be greeting the idea with enthusiasm rather than sadness.

She tried to push aside all her negative thoughts as she walked into the office while Mr. Darcy held the door for her. She was deliberately trying to think of him as Mr. Darcy again, hoping to squash any deepening feelings, though she knew it was far too late to do so.

"Hello, Mr. and Mrs. Darcy," said Mr. Harry in a booming voice that made Fitzwilliam wince.

Lizzy smiled a little at that, feeling a little meanspirited for enjoying his discomfort, but it was well justified. She told herself that firmly as she sat down.

"Everything is ready for your signatures. All you have to do is return to England to file the paperwork, Mr. Darcy." As he spoke, Mr. Harry sorted two piles of papers, stacked them neatly, and handed first one to Lizzy and the other one to Fitzwilliam. "Please review everything and then sign. I shall sign to confirm that I was a witness, and once Mrs. Darcy has her examination, everything is ready to file. I anticipate you will both be annulled within six months."

Lizzy frowned. "I did not expect it to take that long."

"First, you must account for Mr. Darcy's return to England, and then there is a process there as well. Not only will the magistrate have to sign off on the annulment, but the Archbishop must as well."

Lizzy nodded, understanding the delay now. "Still, we shall be done with each other in half a year. You must be quite happy, Mr. Darcy?" she asked in an arch tone, wondering what his response would be.

He was staring at his paperwork, but his gaze was unfocused. He didn't appear to be seeing the words in front of him. "Half a year?" He repeated that in a questioning tone.

Lizzy frowned. "Yes. As Mr. Harry explained, the process cannot be hastened. I am certain that aggrieves you, but there is nothing to be done."

"I declare, half a year is not nearly enough time." As he spoke, Fitzwilliam pushed aside the papers in front of him without signing them. He turned to Lizzy. "I do not wish to go forward with this."

Lizzy's hand tightened around the quill that she'd been holding near the X where she was supposed to sign. She hadn't yet managed to force her fingers to bring the quill to touch the paper and leave her signature behind. "What is it you wish to forgo, Mr. Darcy?"

"Blast it, Lizzy, I do not wish to have this annulment. I have made a great many faulty assumptions, and I have acted in a hasty fashion. I do not wish to continue to do so. I feel it would be a grave mistake to set you aside."

She dropped the quill as she stared at him. "What exactly are you saying?"

He sighed impatiently. "Must I spell it out?"

"I am afraid I must insist that you do, for I do not know what thoughts are in your mind, Fitzwilliam, and I cannot assume that I do." Her tone was a little fractious in her irritation.

He ran a hand through his carefully coiffed curls, disheveling them completely. "I wish to make you my wife, Lizzy. Does it matter why we are married? Can we not find happiness with each other?"

Lizzy's eyes widened in shock. "Do you truly believe that, Fitzwilliam?"

He nodded, seeming to forget all about the ache in his head in his enthusiasm. "I do." He lunged forward, taking her hands in his in his excitement. "I no longer believe you conspired with your mother. Upon careful consideration, that theory quickly fell apart. I clung to it because it was convenient for me to cast you in the role of villain. If I had recognized that you had been caught up in the moment as well, then I must acknowledge that you are as innocent in this change of circumstances as I was.

"I was not yet ready to contemplate such a thing before, but having spent these last several days with you, and nearly losing you, has changed my perspective." He brought one of her hands to his mouth to kiss the back of it. "I do not wish to lose you in any manner. Will you be my wife, Lizzy? Because you wish to, not because we were compromised and forced into it?"

Lizzy stared at him, scarcely daring to believe his words. Yet, he seemed completely sincere, and he was certainly not the type of man to set up this elaborate prank and then tell her it was all in jest. Slowly, she curved her hand around his before bringing the other one up to cup his cheek. "If you are sincere, I confess I would enjoy a second chance. I believe perhaps we could be happy with each other, though things will never be completely peaceful. We will always argue, Fitzwilliam." There was a hint of warning in her tone. "I will never be the perfect wife that you might be envisioning."

He grinned. "I do not expect perfection. I know you as you are, and I am quite happy with the woman who is my wife. I do not wish for an annulment, or to be separated from you. Instead, I want to build a future with you. If you insist, I will even remain here in the wilds of Ohio, and we will build a life together."

Lizzy's heart skipped a beat again, and her stomach quivered with excitement as she gripped his hand even tighter in her own. "I confess, I would not wish to return to England or be parted for my family, but I know your dear sister is still there. Your life is there as well."

"I can return once or twice a year as needed to deal with business, and if Georgiana wishes, she can join us here. For now, I would like us to remain in one place while we spend the time to get to know each other properly without the stresses of travel, or the intrusions of life in London and at Pemberley. Is that agreeable to you, Lizzy?"

Lizzy nodded her enthusiasm as she squeaked in surprise when Fitzwilliam pulled her into his arms. He firmly planted her on his lap and kissed her soundly, uncaring that Mr. Harry was observing the entire exchange. After a moment, Lizzy forgot all about him as well as she immersed herself in Fitzwilliam's kiss, clinging to him as his arms wrapped tightly around her.

It was only when the lawyer cleared his throat that they finally broke apart, and Lizzy remembered his presence then. She flushed as she looked at him before quickly looking away.

The lawyer just appeared amused, and he was beaming at them. "I take it I can tear up this paperwork then?"

"Indeed, good sir," said Fitzwilliam, his tone ecstatic.

"That is indeed the best outcome then." He smiled at Mr. Darcy. "I shall present you with a bill before you leave, if that is agreeable, Mr. Darcy?"

Fitzwilliam stood up, setting Lizzy on her feet. "Send it to the Biltmore Hotel care of my room. We will be here for at least a few days."

Lizzy's head was whirling as he rushed her from the law office, clearly intent on returning to the hotel. "We shall stay in Cincinnati for a few days?"

"Of course. It is not the ideal location for a honeymoon, but it will certainly suffice."

Lizzy's eyes widened. "Oh, I see. What do you have in mind, Fitzwilliam?"

"Holing up in our room with prodigious amounts of room service to ensure both our continued strength and mitigate the need to leave our bed. Is that agreeable to you, Mrs. Darcy?"

Lizzy beamed. "That is most agreeable indeed, Mr. Darcy."

97

Epilogue

Two years later

"I do believe I see their wagon," said Lizzy with a hint of excitement as she clutched Fitzwilliam's arm.

"I am so looking forward to meeting your friend," said Jane. "If she had not saved you..." Jane trailed off, starting to blink. She was even more emotional now that she was heavily with child, but she somehow managed to stifle the urge to cry.

Lizzy was glad of that, wanting no tears with the Napier family planning to visit for the first time. Circumstances had not aligned to allow them to before, first with Lizzy and Fitzwilliam finding a plot of land and building their own place, and then with Lizzy having an unexpectedly difficult pregnancy with their first child. Now, things were finally settling down, and Rebecca and Françoise were bringing their girls and their son to the Darcy homestead.

As soon as the wagon stopped, Lizzy darted down the stairs. She wasn't particularly worried about a graceful greeting as she rushed to Rebecca and hugged her. When she did so, she realized her friend was expecting again. Adeline and Jeannie were the next down from the wagons, and though Jeannie clearly didn't remember her, Adeline seemed to. Their little brother, Pierre, was hanging back shyly, but Bingley soon won him over by producing a peppermint candy.

As the families settled on the porch, the housekeeper brought out pitchers of lemonade, and Lizzy lifted little George onto her lap as he toddled over to her. He laid his head on her, probably wanting to nurse, but she was certain he could wait a little bit longer. Instead, she focused on visiting with her friends and enjoying the contentment of the moment as she gently rocked her son.

"You seem quite happy here," said Françoise to Fitzwilliam sometime after the visit had begun.

Fitzwilliam was rocking slowly in his chair. "Surprisingly, I am. It is quite different from life at Pemberley, but I trust Georgiana's husband to be in charge of that. They expect to come visit us sometime this summer again, and it will be nice to see my sister once more."

"Might she stay?" asked Rebecca.

"I doubt it," said Fitzwilliam. He sounded vaguely sad about that. "She likes our home in small amounts, but she prefers London or Pemberley. It works out quite nicely though, for she and Simon can oversee the management of Pemberley, freeing me for my attention and devotion to my family here."

"She is such a dear girl," said Jane, who had fallen into conversation easily with Rebecca, as though they had been friends forever. "It would be lovely to have her nearby, but she seems most content in England."

"We must be where we are happy," said Lizzy, feeling philosophical for a moment. She contemplated what had brought her to these circumstances in life, wondering how things would have changed if she had stayed in England instead of coming along with Kitty when she married Jacob.

She didn't wish to contemplate that, for she doubted any circumstances would have existed that would have brought her and Fitzwilliam close the way they were now. Their marriage would have been annulled, and that would have been the end of it. She would have never known the kind of happiness she would miss out on, so perhaps she wouldn't have cared, but knowing what she knew now, the idea made her ache, and she was relieved she had taken the path she had. She was even more relieved that Fitzwilliam had been stubborn enough to follow behind her, at first ready to shed himself of his runaway bride, but his sense had prevailed.

"You seem quite happy," said Rebecca a short time later, whispering in a low tone.

Lizzy smiled as she cuddled her son and glanced at her husband for a moment before looking back at her friend and nodding. "I am quite content."

"I told you he did not look at you like a man who wished to be rid of you. Now, he looks at you like you are the center of his world."

Lizzy grinned at that. "It is only fair, for I fear he is at the center of mine as well. To have it any other way would feel quite unnatural."

Rebecca nodded her agreement, and Jane gave a small sigh that indicated she agreed as well. She was clearly as happy with Bingley as Lizzy was with Fitzwilliam, and Rebecca was with Françoise. They were all content in their bliss, and Lizzy wouldn't have it any other way.

PLEASE SIGN UP FOR Abbey's newsletter[1] to receive information about new releases. If you have any difficulties, email Abbey to request a manual add.

---

1. https://www.subscribepage.com/JAFF

About The Author

Abbey is a diehard Jane Austen fan and has loved Fitzwilliam since the first time she "met" him at age thirteen upon borrowing the book from the school library. He is the ideal

Did you love *Darcy's Runaway Bride*? Then you should read *Obstinacy & Obligation: A Sweet Pride & Prejudice Variation*[1] by Abbey North!

[2]

Tasked with finding her a husband, he concludes he is the best choice.

When Mr. Bennet collects on an old debt, Fitzwilliam finds himself in the strange position of inviting Lizzy to London on a secret mission to find her a husband. She isn't to know his intentions, per his promise to her father, but as he introduces her to men of the Ton, he finds it increasingly difficult to imagine Lizzy marrying anyone but him. Will she move past her refusal to ever marry and accept his proposal? If she does, how will she react when she learns of the scheme her father invented and he undertook? Can Lizzy get past her obstinacy to see the motivation behind his obligation?

---

1. https://books2read.com/u/3RLpgp

2. https://books2read.com/u/3RLpgp

Also by Abbey North

A Month To Love
Reproach (Part One)
Resentment (Part Two)
Rapport (Part Three)
A Month To Love Compilation

Classic Fusions
The Phantom Of Netherfield
Darcy's Christmas Carol

Crime & Courtship
Rapacity & Rancor
Abduction & Acrimony
Extortion & Enmity
Murder & Misjudgment
Perfidy & Promises
Crime & Courtship

Darcy's Courtesan
Adversity (Darcy's Courtesan, Part One)
Avidity (Darcy's Courtesan, Part Two)
Amity (Darcy's Courtesan, Part Three)
Darcy's Courtesan: A Sensual "Pride & Prejudice" Variation

Darcy Under the Mistletoe
Christmas At Pemberley: A Pride & Prejudice Variation
Darcys' First Christmastide
Mistletoe & Misunderstanding: Sweet "Pride & Prejudice" Variation

Marriage & Mysteries
Honeymoon & Hemlock

Mr. Darcy's Secret Stories
Mistaken Masquerade: A Pride & Prejudice Variation
Mischief & Matchmaking: A "Pride & Prejudice" Variation

Standalone
A Scandalous Proposition: A Pride & Prejudice Variation
A Bundle of Joy: A Sweet "Pride & Prejudice" Variation
Shadow of Darcy: A Sensual Pride & Prejudice Paranormal Variation
Darcy's Obsession
A Baby At Pemberley: A Sweet "Pride & Prejudice" Variation

Blackmailing Lizzy: A "Pride & Prejudice" Variation
A Lingering Melody: A Sweet "Pride & Prejudice" Variation
Darcy's Wicked Game
Puppies & Prostrations: A Sweet "Pride & Prejudice" Variation
Danger With Darcy: A Sensual "Pride & Prejudice" Variation
Passion & Prostrations: A Sensual "Pride & Prejudice" Variation
Darcy's Debt: A Sensual Pride & Prejudice Variation
In Good Time: A Sweet "Pride & Prejudice" Variation
Obstinacy & Obligation: A Sweet Pride & Prejudice Variation
A Secret Admirer: A Sweet "Pride & Prejudice" Variation
Follies & Foibles: A Sweet "Pride & Prejudice" Variation
Fortune & Misfortune: A Sweet "Pride & Prejudice" Variation
Heartsick: A Sweet "Pride & Prejudice" Variation
Ruination at Ramgsate: A Sweet "Pride & Prejudice" Variation
A Wicked Scheme: A Mystery Romance "Pride & Prejudice" Variation
Darcy's Alibi: A Sweet "Pride & Prejudice" Variation
Darcy's Runaway Bride
Never A Bride: A Fade-To-Black "Pride & Prejudice" Variation
Marooned With Darcy: A Sensual "Pride & Prejudice" Variation
Compromising Mr. Darcy: A Steamy "Pride & Prejudice" Variation
Marrying Mr. Darcy: A Sensual "Pride & Prejudice" Variation
To Dance With Darcy

9 798215 207949